CAT GOT YOUR TONGUE

THE CELTIC WITCH MYSTERIES

BOOK FIVE

Molly Milligan

One

Four days before Lughnasadh/Lammas (the first of August)

"How are we going to eat them?" I asked in confusion as my cousin Maddie added a four-pack of baked beans to the already overflowing shopping trolley. The cans wedged themselves between a two-litre bottle of fizzy orange, and a bag of potato crisps so large that once empty, it could double as a bin liner.

"The usual way," she said, dismissively. "You eat them on toast, right? With knives and forks and probably some disgusting British sauce that's only identified by its colour."

"Maddie, we're having a picnic. You do have them in America, don't you? Although maybe they're called something different. I dunno what. Anyway, we're going to be outside. We'll be balancing plastic plates on our knees. Getting grass and twigs in our drinks. Screaming at wasps. The perfect countryside idyll. We have sandwiches and pies and cakes. But what we don't *usually* have is baked beans on toast."

She put the cans back on the shelf with a toss of her head. "Hey, look, I'm only trying to be more British, you know? You guys seem to have them at any time of the day. I went to see Sian a few days ago and she was eating them at midday but I've seen Dilys have them for breakfast and you once tried to make me eat them at night, so I figured, okay, picnics. I mean, you've put some pretty strange stuff in here already." She picked up a packet of scotch eggs between finger and thumb and peered at them with distaste. "You made me eat one of these once, too," she said. Her tone suggested that it was an ongoing and unforgiveable grievance.

I regretted that now. I regretted anything that might have made Maddie dislike Wales or my home town or Llanfair. She'd been staying with me and my Great Aunt Dilys for months now – long enough for her homesickness to settle into a continually subdued festering pain. Or so I imagined it. She never actually mentioned it. But sooner or later, wouldn't she leave? The imminent arrival of her mother meant most of our conversations mentioned her home in California, and I was growing jealous of a place that I had never even been.

She could have beans on toast at a picnic if it meant she would stay here in Wales for a little while longer. As she turned around and moved away, attracted towards a display of fancy jars of chutney, I popped the beans back into the trolley. I'd think of a way to serve them.

"Bronwen Talog," called a low male voice.

I put on my best professional healer face – well, I tried to look less grumpy than usual – and smiled at the trio of men that approached me. I knew them all, at least vaguely. They'd always lived in Llanfair, and I'd always lived here, and so we were aware of one another in that typical small-town way: I could have told you the family tree of each of them, but nothing real and important like what football teams they supported.

"Hey, Owain, John, Evan," I said. Those were three innocuous Welsh names, everyday and interchangeable. But the three men they attached to were less usual. I'd always found them slightly … odd.

And I should know how to recognise "odd." I see it in the mirror every morning.

John Morgan Driscoll, my favourite of the three, didn't speak. He rarely did. In fact he wasn't often seen in company. He was a tall and rangy man with a weathered brown face and eyes so pale and blue that they seemed white against his teak-skin. I often saw him at a distance, walking the hills. He was heavily involved in the protection of birds of prey in the area, and so our paths had occasionally crossed in a professional manner. He gazed at me, and nodded very slightly. He was clutching a box of lager.

Most people in the supermarket were buying similar things. They were either shopping for picnics – like us – or stocking up for a barbecue or summer garden party. Everyone had had a rush of Pimms to the head and wanted to make the most of the balmy August weather before the inevitable encroachment of winter in, oh, about three days' time.

Owain Campbell was the most approachable of the three men. He was the youngest, in his mid-twenties, and he was a builder's mate. If you wanted a quick household job doing, and you didn't mind paying in cash, he'd pop round after a day's work and do little things for you – hush hush – using his boss's tools. His boss undoubtedly knew. He grinned at me and then winked towards Maddie. "She's still here, then?"

"No, that's just her shadow she left behind," I said.

Evan Morley – the third man and the one I really didn't like – hissed and stared intently at me, like I'd said something important. "Don't joke, though, eh?" he said.

Evan Morley was in his late thirties, a perpetual singleton with flaky skin and slightly bulging eyes. He smelled sickly-sweet and I knew there was some medical issue that lingered, but he didn't seem to seek help for whatever it was. I tried not to let that cloud my impression of him. After all, I dealt with ill people all the time.

But he was different. The illness ran through him like a stick of rock.

I summoned up all my compassion and smiled. "Sorry. So, are you guys having a party?"

Owain looked at our overflowing trolley and said, "Reckon we might join yours!"

I would have run away and hidden in a box but at that point the paragon of neighbourly kindness that was Maddie appeared. I made a quick round of introductions.

Owain lingered as he shook her hand, rather too formally, but it delighted her. There was a definite mutual simpering going on. He was young and fit, and so was she. In all senses of the word. She developed a new crush just about every other week, and I was kinda jealous of that ability to find pure pleasure in obsessing over someone else from a distance. My obsessions were less innocent.

I was about to roll my eyes but then I noticed that Evan Morley was also rolling his eyes so I decided to be the bigger person, and I smiled instead. "Come on," I said to Maddie, "We'd best get on to the check-outs and pay for this lot."

"Oh, wait, no," she said. "I forgot something. We can make sushi rolls, right?" She darted off.

"That's raw fish, isn't it?" Evan muttered.

"I like sushi," Owain declared, which confirmed to me that he definitely had the hots for Maddie. And of the three, he was most certainly the best choice.

I wanted to show Maddie how nice and neighbourly I could be.

And wouldn't it be good if she had more reasons to stay in Llanfair?

"Hey," I said. "If you guys did want to come and try the sushi, we're having a kind of picnic in the garden tomorrow afternoon, so call in if you like."

"Oh, nah," Evan started to say, but Owain hushed him.

"Sure, we might come and say hi. Is it a big thing, like?"

"No, it's just us and Aunt Dilys and … well, it's to celebrate Maddie's mum coming over for a visit. My aunt Ceri."

Evan blinked rapidly. John and Owain went still. All three fixed me intently.

"Your aunt?"

"Maddie is my cousin," I said. It was something I was used

to explaining. "Did you not realise? Her mum is my mum's sister – she married an African-American man and has been over in the USA for decades now. But she's coming to see us all, for the first time in forever."

"Your mum was Lowri Talog," Evan said slowly.

"Yes. Yes, she *is*." I didn't like the past tense. She had been dead for many years. But she was still my mum. That had never stopped. "Everyone knows that."

Evan turned to John and frowned.

I knew what was bothering him. Maddie's darker skin and tightly-spiralled hair next to my paleness and poker-straight tresses – but you could tell we were cousins when you looked at our eyes.

Clearly, these men were not looking at our eyes.

I sighed. I didn't have time for any social crusades right now. I pushed my trolley past them and not one of them said goodbye.

***

I caught up with Maddie at the checkouts and she didn't mention the three men, so nor did I. We loaded ourselves up with the groceries and began a slow walk back through town to our long, low cottage on the far side of Llanfair.

"Hey, you're quiet. Are you looking forward to meeting my mom?"

No, I thought. *Not really*. "Of course," I said. But I owed Maddie honesty. It was just hard to be honest even with myself.

Still, I tried. "She's your mam, though, and … it is going to be strange for me."

"Oh my gosh. Do you mean because I have my mom and you don't?"

A lump formed in my throat. I cough-laughed to clear it. "You know, until you said that, I don't think I had even thought of that. She died so long ago that I thought I'd got used to being the orphan. It doesn't usually bother me when people talk about their own parents. So please don't worry about that."

"Yeah but it could still be awkward," she said.

"If it is, that's my fault and no one else's," I assured her. "God, it's hot, isn't it?"

"Hmm," she said.

"I know, I know, it's nothing like California. Ugh. But you have air-conditioning and all that."

"Yeah but not outside."

"I'm sure that's only a matter of time," I said. Sweat was stinging my eyes now. I shifted the bags but the movement only brought a temporary relief to my painful hands.

But the conversation had also shifted, and that was a much bigger relief.

It wasn't just that Maddie still had her mum, and I didn't.

What was Maddie's mum going to look like?

She was my mum's sister, after all…

And I wasn't sure how I was going to handle that.

***

"Hey," I said once we were nearly home. "So what about that Owain, hey?"

"Yeah, he was cute. Who is he?"

"He's a builder's mate."

"He fixes stuff?"

"Yup. Got anything that you think might want … *fixing?*"

"How do you do that?" Maddie demanded.

"Do what?"

"Make things sound dirty when they aren't dirty. Honestly, you guys. I thought the British were uptight and prudish. But you're all low down filthy smut merchants."

I beamed with pride. "Yes, we are."

We tramped around the side of the cottage. The five-bar gate that should have opened outwards to let us get to the back garden was hanging free of one hinge, and I put my bags down to drag it up and over the gravel.

"You know," I said, "maybe Owain could come around and fix this for us. What do you think?"

Maddie smiled. "You're just trying to set me up now."

"No, it's a practical consideration, that's all. So why don't I go ask him? I'll tell him to come when you're not here, if you're worried. Maybe tomorrow morning when you're at work…"

"No, no," she said. "I don't mind."

"Ha!"

I hauled the gate closed behind me and we went into the back garden. When I say "garden", don't be imagining some beautiful English country scene, all tumbling roses and pretty colours. For a start, this is Wales. And next up, that would take effort and I am busy enough, thank you. We had a cracked set of flagstones we liked to call a patio, steps rising up to a moss-damp lawn, and a riot of herbs and shrubs that harboured all manner of secrets. The right hand wall at the back bordered on to open moorland, and to the left the stone wall marked the boundary between our garden and the graveyard of the small and ill-attended local church.

But this garden was a haven for me, regardless of its mess and chaos. It was my most sacred place, a semi-cultivated retreat of comfort and power.

And today it was full of straw.

Of course it was.

As I fought my way through the ankle-deep morass, my great aunt called, "Put the kettle on while you're in there, love."

I grunted a reply. I kicked open the back door and dragged the shopping bags into the kitchen, followed by Maddie and a scattering of straw that was clinging to our shoes. We quickly got all our purchases stowed away and I brewed up.

"Are you looking forward to your mam coming over, though?" I asked.

Maddie was facing away from me. She nodded, but I could see that pinkness shimmered in the air around her curly hair. She was trying to calm herself with glamour. I went to her side and put my hand on her shoulder. "What's up?"

"What if she wants me to go home?"

"Why would she want that? Anyway, it's your decision."

"She's been saying how much she misses me. But I'm not ready to leave here yet."

"We're not ready to lose you." I squeezed her shoulder. "And you've got a lot of things to do. Your evening classes, your work at Sian's shop, and your imminent seduction of one man called Owain."

"Hush your mouth! Don't you dare say anything to my mom or aunt Dilys."

"What's it worth?"

"I'll … uh, so I'll promise not to swap all your clothes for sparkly and glittery pink dresses. Cos you totally know that I could."

She could. I grimaced. Only the hot weather had persuaded me out of my customary jeans, and I was currently rocking some shapeless yet practical cargo shorts, of a style favoured by dads the world over. I didn't care.

When I went outside again, clutching a tray with cups of tea and plates of biscuits – no, my aunt hadn't asked for the biscuits too but I knew her, and was just saving myself a journey back inside – Dilys was cackling like the stereotypical hag she was trying very hard to be.

"What do you think?" she asked. She was holding up a homemade scarecrow that was taller than she was. She'd taken a pair of old jeans, and stiffened them with broom handles before stuffing them with straw. The upper body was a tweed jacket over a stuffed pillowcase, and the head was currently another pillowcase with a crudely drawn face on it.

"I think I am going to have nightmares," I said as I set the tray down on a white plastic chair. "The scarecrow festival is for all ages, you know. It's a family thing. This isn't some adults-only horror event. You'll get banned if you turn up with that."

"I don't know what you mean," she said huffily. "This is a classic scarecrow, this is. You young people today are too sensitive. In my childhood, we couldn't afford to have feelings so they never got hurt."

Maddie stepped in, ever the peace-maker. She didn't dare use her Fair Folk-inspired glamour on Aunt Dilys – that would have ended badly for all concerned – but she spoke in a soothing voice. "It sure has presence," she said. "I mean, the clothes are great and all. But, you know, I just think the face could do with a little work. You've made a good start but I'm thinking maybe more realistic features?"

"And less the stuff of demons and darkness?" I added. "That would be good."

"Lipstick, then," Dilys said. "I'll go over his mouth with some lipstick."

Both Maddie and I sucked in deep breaths and looked at one another, unsure of how to tell Dilys that was only going to make things worse. Luckily, we were interrupted by Dean.

Dean's the local druid. He's a young man of gangling limbs and nerdy looks, with a simmering and not-very-secret crush on Maddie. It's a very pure and courtly flame that he holds for her. I personally think he enjoys being besotted with her, and would not want to go any further than that. He likes being in thrall to the idea of Maddie.

"I … good god. What in all the names of deities past and present is *that*?" he asked. He squinted forward at the apparition and then shuddered, stepping back.

"This is my entry to the scarecrow competition," Dilys said.

"But why? Llanfair has been a good home to you."

"Don't you start. None of you appreciate my artistic genius."

Dean shivered again. He bent and picked up a handful of straw. "Did you intercept a delivery that was supposed to be going to a stable-yard?" he asked. "How many are you making? An army?"

I think we all shivered at the idea of such an army of terror.

"I know people, that's all," Dilys said defensively. "People often owe me favours for … things I have done for them. I might have ended up with more straw than I needed, but it's all good."

Dean shook his head. "Do you know definitely where this came from?"

"A field," she snapped. "I don't know which one. Why does it matter?"

"It is lammas-time," he said. "Lughnasadh. Of course it matters. This is John Barleycorn himself, remember."

"I remember."

"And so does he," Dean said, letting the pale stalks drop through his fingers to the ground. "John Barleycorn has memories too, you know."

We tried to laugh it off but when we got to our cups of tea, they had all gone cold.

Two

There was some confusion on just when Ceri, Bron's mum, was supposed to arrive. I hadn't been party to most of the arrangements, partly because a lot of the information and organisation was done online. I have a bit of an issue with electrics; unless I am very careful, I blow things up. We've just about got working electricity in the house, but wifi has proved to be impossible. In fact, our neighbours complain from time to time; when I get angry or upset, their router resets.

But she didn't come that day, and I ignored the straw-filled menace in the garden, and got on with my usual day to day healing tasks. Dilys said that she thought she was landing late that night, and would make her way from the airport to Llanfair early the next morning. Maddie went to spend the rest of the afternoon at Sian Pederi's shop in town, and I was happy being left alone with just my cat, Harkin, for company as I worked.

I made up some potions and lotions to put aside. Illnesses generally ran in seasonal waves and I knew I'd need lots of creams for bites, stings and sunburn, soothing draughts for hay-fever, and poultices ready for the inevitable slew of strains and sprains as semi-drunk people decided that dancing in the middle of the road or climbing a tree was a great idea.

I went out to deliver a few things, and got stuck in the gate again. It made me think of Maddie and Owain. He hung around with some strange men – well, John was okay but that Evan was a leering sort – but Owain himself seemed fine. So it made sense, to my mind, to look for Owain while I was in town doing my errands, and ask him to stop by that evening, to fix our gate. He readily agreed.

I was hugely pleased with my matchmaking efforts. It all went like clockwork. We were sitting down in the evening when there was a knock at the back door and Owain shoved his head in, calling out a cheery greeting. Maddie jumped up and I acted very casual, but did not dare to meet Dilys's eye. And no one could disagree that the gate really did need fixing; he'd noticed how bad it was as he came through to the back of the house.

I went outside and Maddie followed. When I came back in to make Owain a cup of tea while he worked, Maddie remained outside with him. I grinned to myself as I set about the kettle.

Dilys was giving me the stink-eye.

"If you put as much effort into your own relationship as you have done with messing with someone else's, the things that are going to happen won't happen," she intoned.

She's a seer. That's a perfectly logical statement for someone like her to make.

I objected anyway. "But if you've seen them, they are going to happen anyway."

"Fate isn't as fixed as that."

"Um, isn't that the whole point of fate?"

"Adam called this morning."

"Did he leave a message?"

Dilys scrunched up her face as if she was trying to remember. I jogged her memory by reaching for the gin bottle and pouring her a small glass of it.

"Lemon too," she instructed.

I chopped a slice of lemon and added the barest token splash of tonic water. "Ah, I remember," she said happily after a sip of her drink. "He said he had been trying to find you and wondered if you wanted to go out for a meal. I told him about the picnic tomorrow afternoon and invited him on your behalf. You're welcome," she added.

"I assumed he would come," I said.

"And there is your problem."

I was saved from any further schooling by Maddie coming back into the house, and she was smiling.

"I've got his brew here," I said. "Do you want to take it to him?"

"He's done, and he's gone."

"That was quick! I haven't paid him."

"He said it was such an easy job that there was no charge."

"Did you glamour him?" I asked her suspiciously.

She just beamed.

***

The next morning, though, there was a new air in the house.

Dilys was dressed in her very best layers of black, and Maddie was trying to clean the range in the kitchen.

"Have you heard from your mam?" I asked.

"Yeah! She's gonna get a cab from the airport," Maddie said.

"But the airport is in England," I said. "Has she won the lottery?"

Maddie just shrugged. "Mom is a force," she said. "She'll get a deal."

I knew that Maddie's mum had no magical ability – according to Maddie, and family legend anyway – but that word choice of 'force' made me feel chilly. I didn't have any more time to reflect on it because I was called to the back door by a knocking from a very frantic young boy, instructing me to come to a local veterinary surgery.

I waved goodbye to Maddie, and followed the boy via the surgery and out to the fields where a deer had become trapped in a fence.

I work well with the local vets. After all, we have the same aims – animal welfare. I was greeted by Bill who was about a hundred years old with three hundred years' worth of experience.

"I could tranquillise her, see," he explained, as the terrified deer twisted in the wire. "But then what use is that to her, after? I'll not be taking her back to the surgery. Last deer I had in my van kicked hell out of the side panels, she did. Anyway, she has no other injuries. So if you could … you know, do what you do, and we can get her free then, me and Ian."

Ian turned out to be a local farmer.

I set about "doing what I do", which in this instance was just a quick mental circle of protection, a brief call to the spirits of place to assist me if they could, and then a gentle psychic communion with the panicking deer.

It took a while to calm her, and a little while longer to clip her free of the fence and to check her for injuries. Then I was called to another job, this time a human one, and so on it went, with half my day ending up being swallowed by this and that.

As I went, I reflected on Maddie and our relationship. I was a solitary curmudgeon and she'd made me recognise that actually, being social and nice was okay too. When she'd first arrived, I'd spent a lot of time trying to be a good host. Now we took one another for granted.

And that was wrong. My eye caught a poster on a lamp post, advertising something that I thought might be a great evening out, and I made a mental note of it.

Maddie liked music, didn't she? I bet she'd love some traditional folk music in a pub.

I hugged the surprise to my chest and carried on my errands.

It was mid-afternoon when I made my way home, carrying the payments for my labour – some bedding and food for the animals in my care, a fruit pie, an antique map of Cornwall (don't ask) and a bottle of suspiciously cloudy homebrew from Mr Carr, who handed it over with a wink and a cough and an ominous instruction to "sip it by the spoon, don't try to drink it by the glass. Good luck."

I knew that Ceri had arrived as soon as I stepped into the back garden. I could feel her presence. No, it was definitely not a magical one. She was human, but she was hugely human – she throbbed with good, solid, down-to-earth energy. A force, as Maddie had said.

I went carefully into the utility room and deposited my gains on a table. I took a moment to breath and steady myself before walking into the kitchen itself.

Ceri stood up.

She was my mother but she was not my mother – she'd had plastic surgery to shave off the bump from her aquiline nose, and she had a Californian tan that contrasted with her sun-bleached blonde hair. No one in Wales ever achieved that look without resorting to hairdressers and sunbeds, and all that did was make us look orangey-pink. She was many years younger than my mother, but as I had lost her so long ago, I fancied that I was seeing her all over again.

But Ceri's expression was mirroring my own discomfort, and I had not expected that at all.

"Bronwen," she said, trying to smile, and sounding so American – so like Maddie – that it helped, actually. This was not my Welsh mother.

"Bron, please," I said, and hovered awkwardly. "Hi." Did she want a hug? I didn't think I ought to put my hand out to her and ask for a handshake.

Maddie stepped in, and virtually threw us together, with a firm hand placed in the smalls of our backs, thrusting us into a collision. Ceri's warm arms went around me and there was a roaring in my ears. Then she stepped back.

"Oh, Bron," she whispered. "You are the image of your

mother. I … wow."

There was a painful pause.

Our mutual discomfort was obvious to everyone.

Maddie linked her arm into her mother's. "Mom, hey, you should see the garden."

"I saw it as I came in."

"Sure, but come see it again. You gotta see the view."

"I know the view. I grew up here…"

Maddie towed her mother out of the kitchen.

I looked at Dilys.

My elderly great aunt looked back at me, and there was a sadness in her rheumy eyes. "It's hard for the both of you, isn't it?"

"Yeah. I hadn't thought about what it was going to be like for her. Just myself. She seems nice. I'm a selfish idiot. Dilys, were she and my mother close?"

Dilys shook her head. "No, no, Lowri and Ceri, they were never seen together, really. But that's no surprise, is it? There was a fifteen year age gap, like."

"But they were sisters."

"They were. Look, though, I was away, you know? Your mother – Lowri – she was born in 1950 and I was her aunt but I was travelling the world. And that was it, you know. I came back from time to time, saw Lowri, saw the family. It was just those three, Lowri and her mum and her dad. Until Ceri was born, suddenly, when Lowri was fifteen already. She was a teenager, you know? She didn't want some baby and then some toddler hanging around. Lowri had left home by the time that

Ceri started school. She was married at twenty, you know, your mother."

"But she didn't have me until she was much older. Why was that? Was she waiting or…"

"It just didn't happen," Dilys said. "It didn't happen. Until it suddenly did, when they'd given up all hope. But Ceri had gone to America by then, you know. So."

I rubbed my temples. If you're confused, don't worry. Sometimes my own family confused me, too; I think it was the generations that were all mixed up. "She definitely doesn't have any magic, though," I said. "Have you ever met Maddie's father?"

"I did the once, yes. He is a lovely man."

"Does he have magic?"

"He has a power that is unfamiliar to me," Dilys said. "I don't know. I wish …"

"What?"

"I wish he had come over for a holiday too."

"I know," I said. "I would have liked to have met him. But he couldn't leave his job."

"His job, yes. They don't get proper holidays in America, do they? But I have a feeling we have a need of power."

I didn't like my aunt to express nervousness. It unsettled me. I patted her on the forearm. "Hush, now, you're still just upset about the scarecrows. Everything will be all right. Shall we start setting up for the food?"

She grinned, a face full of creases. "Yes, let's do something useful. Does Maddie really want beans on toast? With brown sauce or red?"

***

I was glad to throw myself into more work. Maddie came back in and helped us. After a little while, though, I noticed that Ceri was absent.

I slipped out of the kitchen and into the cooler, quieter inner hallway. This had always been our family home. When Maddie had first come her, she'd been keen to know all the details – she'd practically demanded a full family tree and a run-down of each generation of the family. She had been disappointed to discover that we had a pretty lax attitude to our heritage and couldn't actually name anyone much beyond "mad Bert who fought in the war" especially as we weren't sure which war.

I listened to the house breathe. Its protection was curled around a figure upstairs. I made sure to walk heavily as I didn't want to surprise her. I found her sitting on a wooden chair that stood outside the bathroom door. When Dilys was in there, in one of her legendary baths, you needed to have somewhere to sit while you waited for her to emerge.

"Hey," I said, and she looked up. "We made up a room for you."

"I know. But I don't want to go in," she said.

"What's wrong? Has Harkin…"

"No, no, there's nothing wrong. Well, it was … your mom's room."

"Mom? Mam."

She laughed a little. "Yeah, I guess I sound totally

Americanised to you. The thing is, I've lived there longer than I ever lived here."

"But I didn't think a childhood accent would ever leave."

"No, it doesn't, not really, and any of my American friends would tell you I sound very Welsh." She pushed her hair out of her eyes. "I'm sorry. I'm so tired, with jetlag, and it's so strange coming here. Coming home. I shouldn't even call it home any more. It's not my home."

"It will always be a home for you," I assured her. "I'm sorry if I acted weird when I first saw you. I thought I was seeing my mam."

"And when I saw you, that's what I thought, too. I'm shocked with myself, if I'm honest. I didn't think it would be so hard to come here."

"But it's all good memories, right?" I asked her.

She looked at me with sad eyes. "No." Then she shook herself and forced a bright, sunny and false smile back onto her face. "But I am *so* glad to see Maddie's settled in! Thank you so much for looking after her and all!"

"You're welcome," I said, somewhat taken aback by the sudden all-American onslaught of emotion. "She's working part time, but of course she can't get paid for it, but Sian is teaching her all about the Fair Folk, and she's taking evening classes…"

"I know, she told me! I am so proud of her. And you. And everyone. It's so good to be here!"

She was lying. But I didn't call her out on it. She looked exhausted and we were about to spring a picnic on her? I said, "Hey, we've only just started doing the food. If you want to just crash out in bed, we'll do this tomorrow. We can shove it all in the fridge."

"No, not at all!" She jumped to her feet and linked her arm into mine, just the way that Maddie did. "Come on. I'm hiding up here when I should be helping out in the kitchen, right?"

I couldn't persuade her to rest. We marched down the stairs and back to join the others.

***

It was nice. Honestly, the picnic started off really nice.

You'll note that word *started.*

The sun was out. We had shade under the trees. We had a long table set out with the food and drink, and a bucket of cold water keeping things cool. Harkin wove around, and birds sang lazily in the branches. Somewhere, a sheep was calling.

And the conversation began to flow.

Ceri talked about what was happening back in the place that Maddie had come from. I didn't mind the exclusion, really. I half-listened and fully-ate, and enjoyed the warmth of the sun. It was good to hear Maddie laugh, and I grew more relaxed again in Ceri's presence. She was hiding something and it was causing her pain, but at this moment, it didn't matter.

Maddie began to complain of a headache, but she waved away any offers of help. I said I could heal her, and Dilys offered some brandy. "It's only the excitement," she said. "I haven't slept well lately."

No wonder, I supposed, with her mother coming over. I

put it out of my mind. And then Adam, my boyfriend, turned up and there was another rash of introductions and explanations.

He grinned hello to me, but he moved on quickly, and that was understandable, but Dilys nudged me and hissed. I ignored her.

Adam charmed Ceri; everyone had a soft spot for a cheerful young policeman, it seemed. He had grown up in West Africa and could talk about the experience of travel and moving to a new country with both Ceri and Maddie. Even my aunt had her own globetrotter's tales to spin, having spent much of her youth getting arrested around the world. I suspected the British Foreign Office had a whole file on her. Me, I had nothing but the land below me, anchoring me in ways that could never be fully explained. I didn't mind that I had never left, and would never leave, this place. In fact I thought that Adam and Ceri ought to envy me, because they were missing out on roots.

Roots didn't just form in space, but also in time.

Ceri seemed to realise that their chatter about travel was leaving me out. She tried to include me, saying, "You're welcome to come over and stay with us, you know, Bron!"

"Oh, no, but thank you," I said.

"Come on. You can't stay in Wales all your life."

"Of course I can! This is my home."

"Well, it was my home too, but you can make new ones. Anyway, I don't even mean that," Ceri said. "I'm not saying come and live with us. Just come and visit."

I shook my head. "It's not really my thing."

She frowned at me and even Dilys tutted. Too late, I realised this was one of those situations that I was supposed to lie about – social convention meant I should be saying, "Oh I would love to!" and that would be that. Everyone would know that I didn't really mean it.

"One day I'm going to whisk you away," said Adam.

Ceri giggled at that blatant flirting but I was embarrassed and looked away. "Does anyone want more lemonade? Just me? Back in a minute."

I escaped back into the house and Adam followed me. "Are you all right?" he asked as we went into the utility room.

"Yeah. Sorry. Just a bit unsettled, that's all. Adam, she looks like old photos of my mam."

He enfolded me in a warm hug. "It's okay. I can't imagine how strange it must be for you. I came looking for you earlier."

"Dilys said. I've been busy."

"I know. But I really want to take you out and talk through some of the stuff I've been learning about."

Adam, who had not a scrap of magical ability, had been trying to read up on the various paths and spiritual practices of the world. I loved the fact that he was interested enough to make an effort, but I sometimes caught him looking at me oddly. A little knowledge was a dangerous thing, and I wondered what he was learning that was making him wary of me.

"I'm always happy for you to take me out," I said. "But it's a really mad time at the moment."

"I know." He sighed heavily. "Come on. Did you really want lemonade?"

I did, and I grabbed a fresh bottle from the fridge.

He knew what it was like for me, with busy days and everything, I thought, and let a slight annoyance cloud my mind as I followed him back out into the garden. And I think he was still a little annoyed himself, because he walked stiff-backed towards the others and sat down heavily on a plastic chair, turning to speak to Maddie rather than me.

There was no time to soothe the waters, though, because suddenly we heard a gaggle of voices coming around the side of the house.

"We're here!" the horrible rat-like Evan declared, hoisting a cardboard box aloft. The contents slid and thudded dully; it was a packed crate of beer cans. He was followed by Owain, who had brought a large two-litre bottle of the cheapest, nastiest cider possible, with a lurid blue label and dust on the plastic. It had clearly been lingering in a shed, or on the bottom shelf of a corner shop, for too long. John Morgan Driscoll brought up the rear, empty-handed. He scowled. It was a familiar expression and I found that I didn't mind it.

Dilys hauled herself to her feet and grabbed her walking stick. "Adam, arrest them all!" she said, pointing her stick at them. I hoped it wasn't the one with the hidden knife; she claimed to own such a thing, but all my surreptitious searching had not yet unearthed it. And I didn't want to discover which one it was by seeing it in action, disembowelling a neighbour or something.

Adam went to Dilys's side and put a calming hand on her arm, while I got up and grinned awkwardly. I regretted everything, right in that moment. I should never had said anything.

But here they were.

"It's all right," Evan was saying to Adam and Dilys. "She invited us. Didn't you, Bron?"

Maddie pressed a hand to her forehead. "I might have to go for that lie-down," she muttered.

That was the last thing that I wanted. The whole point was that I intended to get Owain and Maddie together, properly, somehow, before she got too homesick with her mother's presence, and left us all to return to California.

Adam was glaring at me. "Bron?"

"So, yeah, I kinda mentioned it to them when I saw them yesterday in the shops," I said, feeling my cheeks burn. "I was being polite and neighbourly."

"You?"

"Yeah, me," I snapped back at him, though he didn't deserve it. "I can actually be a nice person, actually, you know, sometimes, actually."

I sounded like an idiot. Adam sighed. I was making him do a lot of sighing lately, it seemed.

Evan pushed past Adam and plonked himself down in a spare plastic chair. He ripped open the cardboard container and pulled out a can of lager. He popped the ring-pull and took a deep drink, spilling a great deal of it on his chin.

"But did you properly invite them?" he asked again, incredulous.

"I did," I said, and my eyes flicked to Maddie, and she suddenly coloured and flared her nostrils at me.

She knew what I'd done, and why. She was going to get me alone, and kill me. Yes, she liked Owain, but this was too public.

She's literally kill me for this. But she'd do it really politely, and apologise while she did it, because this was Maddie after all.

John, still at the back, put his empty hands in his pockets, and muttered, "Yeah, we shouldn't be here. We'll go. We got the wrong end of the stick. Owain, Evan. C'mon."

Owain looked nervously at Maddie. "Hey. Is the gate working okay?"

"Um, yeah. Thanks."

Well, so that was going well.

Evan grabbed a can out of the box resting on his knees, and stared directly at Ceri. "You are Bron's mum's sister, then, are you?"

"I am. Ceri," she said. "Pleased to meet you."

"Really." Evan said it flatly. "Are you? Pleased to meet *us?*"

He got to his feet, shoving the box of cans onto the ground.

He stared hard at Ceri with curiosity in his eyes.

Then he looked at Maddie.

What did he mean? I felt a rising anger in my belly.

Owain put up his hand as if to ward someone or something off.

John stepped forward.

And everything happened in a flash.

Evan turned around and Owain leaned forward and someone arced an arm around, and then there was a flash and a bang which made my ears ring. All noise receded into a high-pitched whine, with just underwater echoes as people spoke or screamed.

My eyes had been blinded and I blinked but thick smoke

was filling the air. The barbecue exploded, then, a shower of sparks hissing and screeching like fireworks going on at ground level.

I was on my knees, coughing, aware of sparks fizzing and hissing in the dry grass. Adam, with more presence of mind, threw the bucket of cool water across the barbecue and the surrounding area. More smoke plumed, and we were all retching.

There was a scuffle, and a cry, and a door slammed, and the sound of feet on the gravel, and the gate crashing closed. I hoped Owain's repair would hold up.

It was a minute before the smoke cleared.

And then only me, and Ceri, and Dilys, and John, and Adam remained, coughing.

Three

"What on earth was that?" Ceri demanded.

Adam was staring at the smouldering remnants of the barbecue. "It smells like fireworks to me. What are you playing at, John?"

"Hey, don't blame me. If it were me, would I still be here? You want to go and ask that Evan."

"Owain has gone too," Dilys said.

"And Maddie," Ceri said, and she sounded high-pitched and scared.

I rubbed at my face. "John Morgan, you're an idiot."

He almost laughed at me. "Owain was making eyes at your Maddie, and she was making eyes back. So that's the long and short of it, isn't it? You really just wanted him to turn up. Not me and Evan too. And now Evan's tried to be funny."

"Well, no one's laughing, are they?" I snapped. "Did you know what he was going to do? This was planned."

John shrugged. "Evan doesn't plan further than his next meal," he said. "But yeah, he talking about it. I told him not to, you know, but he thought it would be funny. Liven things up, you know? Anyway. Sorry about all that. You might as well keep the beer. I'll go catch up with Evan. I suppose Owain has nipped off with your Maddie. So, bit of a result for you, then. That's what you wanted. See you." He sloped off, kicking at the gravel, as casual as you please.

"Fireworks?" I said, looking to Adam to explain everything. In fact, we all were. "Really?"

He sighed and poked at the smouldering, sticky black mess of ash where the barbecue had been. "Yeah, it looks like it. I don't know where they'd get them at this time of year. Maybe it was stuff they had left over, but who keeps fireworks around? But yeah, that was all it was. Idiots, the lot of them."

"I really am sorry," I said.

"Is there really something between my Maddie and that oaf?" Ceri asked.

"Owain? He's the best of the three and he's not an oaf. He fixed the gate. Yeah, I think they like one another."

Ceri frowned. "I will have something to say about *that*."

"I'm sorry," I said again. "I made a huge mistake. I shouldn't have invited them."

Everyone nodded and no one said anything nice to make me feel better, which was fair enough, really.

Dilys was the only person who hadn't moved from her chair. I suppose when you've lived through a hostage-taking in South America, some idiot chucking fireworks on a barbecue is a mere blip. Ceri was looking pained, with a mixture of fear, trepidation and annoyance on her face, though that could have just been jetlag and dodgy scotch eggs. Adam was tidying up.

That was what I should have started to do.

Instead, I followed John's path out through the gate and stood on the pavement in front of our house. I had hoped to see the three of them, and speak to them, but they had all disappeared now. I took a moment to compose myself and then went back to the garden.

"Did Maddie come back?" I asked as I began to help Adam tidy up. There seemed little point in continuing with the party.

"Did you not see her just now?" Dilys asked. "I thought you must have been following her."

"Yeah, I went to see if I could spot her. I thought she might be there, with Owain, but I couldn't see anyone," I said. "I didn't see her leave."

"So where is she?" Ceri said, dropping a crumpled can into the recycling bin.

"She said she had a headache. She'll probably be inside," I said. But I had heard footsteps on the gravel. Maybe she had gone with Owain, like John had been suggesting. She would definitely be fed up with me.

Dilys, who was helping clear up in a supervisory role by sitting still and pointing at things, got to her feet. "I'll go inside and find her," she said. "Don't you worry. I'll call you, Bron, if she needs you."

"She would need *me*," Ceri said. "I am her mom."

"Yes, of course," I said awkwardly. "She only meant, you know, if she needed healing or something."

"I know what she meant," Ceri said, and she narrowed her eyes at me.

Adam coughed.

Harkin chose that moment to begin to weave around my legs. He was calling to me, signalling that something was not quite right. I was grateful of the excuse to leave the garden, and I headed into the utility room where we housed ill or injured animals that needed care and attention.

But Harkin kept on plaintively bugging me, mewing and whining. The issue was not with any of our current charges. I stopped and crouched down. He came to my hand and pressed his head upwards, not purring. I unfocused and let him into my head.

He was distressed – something was off kilter – but I couldn't tell exactly what. He gave me an impression of absence, and a warning, but that was all.

And those impressions were filtered through my own fears right now. It was impossible to tell what he meant.

Adam sidled into the small room. "Bron, you're behaving very strangely," he said in a low voice. I wanted to fall into his arms and hear him tell me that everything was going to be all right.

But I stayed where I was.

And he said, "You know, Ceri's not feeling very well herself. She probably has jetlag. You don't know what that's like but believe me, it's more than feeling a bit woozy. So be nice to her, all right?"

"I am being nice to her!" I said indignantly. So I'd never had jetlag, and everyone else had. Yeah. I was the stick-at-home. I could have had a very petulant and childish rant. I was proud of myself that I didn't. But I did say, "This picnic, everything – this is all for her!"

"And inviting the gatecrashers?"

"They can't be both gatecrashers *and* invited," I snapped. "They weren't gatecrashers really, because I *had* invited them. And I accept I shouldn't have been matchmaking but Owain likes Maddie and Maddie likes Owain, so that's not a bad thing."

"You know what I mean," Adam said. "It didn't pan out the way you expected, I suppose. That happens. But this thing you have with Ceri, whatever it is, you have to let that go."

"There is no thing! I don't know what you're on about."

"Maybe, maybe not. But from the outside, it does look at if you are picking at her. And she doesn't feel very comfortable around you, so I thought you might have said something that I didn't know about."

"Of course I haven't," I said. "I'm appalled. She is my aunt, for heaven's sake. And I have only just met her."

He looked at me like he wanted me to say something else, and I was starting to feel pretty persecuted. Yes, I had messed up by inviting those three men but hey, I could forgive myself that if everyone else could let it go. As for my "issue" with Ceri, I felt as much tension coming from her that was directed right at me. I wasn't getting at her. I was defending myself from her.

What was I supposed to do, keep on apologising?

Maybe the heat was getting to us all. I tried a small smile, and then went past him, out into the garden. I noticed that he pulled back to let me go past, and we didn't touch. Time was when it would have been an excuse for physical contact.

And outside, Ceri was crying. I hadn't expected to see that, and I stopped for a moment.

Harkin was still warning me about something, and I went cold. I broke free of my torpor and raced up to Ceri. She was shaking, and holding a lock of Maddie's hair in her hand. Dilys came out behind me and said what I think we already knew:

"Maddie's not in the house, not anywhere. I even checked the towel cupboard and behind the settee. I did find a bag of crisps, though," she added with a touch of glee. She caught my look, and said defensively, "I've eaten them now."

"I wasn't going to ask you to share," I said, shuddering to think how old they must have been. "Has she left a note or anything?"

"Not a sausage."

Ceri was still shaking, and she said through her tears, "She's been taken, she's been taken, can't you see?"

"She can't have gone from here," I said. "She might have wandered off, to clear her head, or she might have gone with Owain, but she can't have been forcibly *taken*. This garden is protected."

"I can't see any six foot fence," Ceri said.

"No but it's protected by our spirits of place, and also, because of her affinity with the Fair Folk," I pointed out.

Ceri's lip sneered. She was so like Maddie but so unlike her, too, in this bitter ugliness. "No fairy ever stopped a bullet," she said.

"No, but they could glamour the gunman so they didn't shoot at all," I said.

She tipped her head back and gave a howl of frustrated rage to the sky. "God, you people are impossible. This is why I left Wales."

"Is it?"

There was a silence.

Then she said, quite out of the blue, "Did anyone see a polecat here?"

I almost laughed. "There are only cats, two hedgehogs and a bird in the utility room."

"I didn't mean that. It's important." Her voice rose, and her tears fell faster. She shook the lock of hair. Her anger gave way to panic. "Did anyone see a polecat? Where is she? Those men *took* her, you mark my words. Why is this here? What happened? Was there a struggle? She had a headache – she would not have gone off with that Owain. Where did they go? Where do they live? Adam, didn't Dilys tell you to arrest them?"

"Come on, now, let's just be sensible and calm down," Adam said. "We'll find Maddie. She'll be walking, just like Bron said. Let's go and find her, okay?"

"You don't understand," Ceri gabbled. "I'll go after her. She's my daughter." She gripped the lock of curly black hair in her hand. "Oh, I had a bad feeling about all of this. Why didn't I listen?"

Adam had adopted his professional, calming voice. "We will all go together."

Ceri didn't seem to hear him, or she was ignoring him. She ran, curving around the edge of the cottage and through the gravelled parking area.

I followed, and half-turned back, saying to Adam, "Look after Dilys. Please!"

He shouted something after me but I, too, did not hear him.

Ceri had a fair turn of speed on her. I was not one of nature's athletes – in spite of Maddie's attempts to introduce me to "intervals" and "high-intensity training" and "vegetables" – but I did manage to catch up with Ceri by the junction of our road with the minor road that led to the church.

"Wait, I'll help," I gasped. "It will have all changed since you lived here. You'll get lost."

She turned to me, green eyes wet with tears, and said, "When I find the polecat, it will be all right. You'll see. I have my tree. And I can't get lost, not here."

"You've been away –"

"No," she insisted. "It's all the same, it's always going to be the same. Underneath."

She darted away.

And I followed.

Four

I lost her pretty quickly. Partly that was because she was fitter than I was, and that was a frankly embarrassing thought. But in my defence, the town was busy with people milling around in that loud and aimless way they have on hot days. There were tourists, and of course the kids were off school so the market square was packed with hordes of feral children and holidaymakers, and general layabouts with nothing better to do than drink from midday onwards.

I ground to a halt outside Caffi Cwtch. Alston, the owner, had made the barest nod to the summer atmosphere by putting two round tables out on the pavement to cause congestion for pedestrians. The air of casual continental glamour was somewhat marred by the presence, on one of the tables, of Billy, our local down-and-nearly-out. The skinny, red-faced man hailed me.

"Hey, Bron, well then! You look fit to drop."

I gave up the hunt, at least temporarily. There was little to be gained from aimless wandering. I sat down opposite Billy and got my breath back. "It's the heat," I lied.

He snickered a laugh. "Who are you running from? Or are

you running towards something? A pie, maybe?"

I huffed at him. "Ha ha, very funny. Listen, have you seen Maddie go past?"

"Not today, no."

"Do you know her mum? Ceri? She's come over for a visit. Tall, blonde hair, green eyes like me and Maddie both have…"

"Yeah, yeah, I know her. Of course I do. I've been here all my life." He was easily in his fifties, and some days looked twice that age. "I remember her from way back, don't I?"

"Have you seen her go past just now?"

Billy sat back. His scrawny arms were lined and wrinkled, with faint blue tattoos writhing under the papery skin. He scratched his ear with a disconcertingly loud sound. "I have not," he said at last.

"What's up? What do you know about Ceri?" I asked. "Do you also remember … my own mother, Lowri?"

He looked me straight in the eye. He didn't usually do that. Billy cultivated a cowed air, generally, aware of his perceived social status and of his vulnerability. But he looked directly at me, and said, "Now you see, this love business, it is a hard thing, Bron."

"What?"

His voice changed and became lighter. "Oh, yeah, well, that's why I've avoided it all my life, see! Who wants the complications?" He laughed, and it was forced. "Stay single, move fast."

"What happened between them?" I asked. "You know, my mam and Ceri. I don't like what's happening here."

"I don't know," he said.

"Yes, you do." I leaned forward, suddenly angry. "Here's the thing. There's stuff that happened, way back, and some people know, and they're keeping secrets, and it's only going to end badly. It's nonsense. I need to know, all right? So my mam and her sister didn't get on? That's normal for sisters. I can handle knowing that. How bad was it? Did one steal the other one's partner? What? Whatever it was, we can get over it. We're all adults now, aren't we?"

Billy was not going to be roused by me. He didn't even twitch at my outburst.

"Go and look to Ceri's tree," he said.

Something about that phrase tugged at me. Ceri herself had spoken of a tree. I narrowed my eyes and it came to me. "No," I said. "You mean Ceridwen's Tree, and that's not the same. My aunt's name is not Ceridwen. Just Ceri."

"Words do change over time. It might be Ceridwen's Tree now, but was it always?"

"I'm guessing not, then." Everyone in the town knew about the thin birch tree that stood alone and stark on the common land near the river. It was unusual for the strips of papery white bark that unfurled from its trunk. It was the only birch tree in the area as far as I knew.

"We remake our histories to suit our present selves," Billy said. Then he closed his eyes and groaned, and thinned his lips.

I thanked him but he didn't see me. I felt a ripple of pain run through him, and a dark confusion in his mind, and I knew he needed to find some alcohol soon. He was an addict of many years. I got up and put my hand over his. He never, ever, asked for my help and it was one of the rules of healing that it shouldn't be given out, unasked for, unsought.

But I let a warmth of relief spread from my chest to his, and if that rule-breaking came back to bite me, then I could deal with the sting, this once.

***

What else was there to do but a little bit more aimless wandering, even though I knew it was pointless? It was better than going home.

I went to the very centre of the town square and let the flow of humanity buffet me. I sat on a bench the moment one became free, and closed my eyes. Maddie would be somewhere here. I knew her. She wouldn't go up into the hills. That was my natural instinct. As an introvert, I would always choose to recharge by seeking solitude and wildness. But she drew her everyday energy from the proximity to other people, and so she'd come here, I reckoned.

I sought her out, feeling for her now-familiar psychic imprint. We were close enough that I should have been able to detect her, even in this crowded space. Her warmth and glamour left a trail.

"Boo!"

I jerked back to awareness as Lacey and her teenage cronies swarmed around me, shoving themselves on to the bench with no regard for my personal space. I hadn't found Maddie, and I certainly wouldn't now, with their crackling energy invading everything.

Lacey nudged me with her elbow. "What's up! Haven't seen you around much."

"Well, no. I think your parents wouldn't be happy about that." We had some unpleasant history, unfortunately.

But Lacey was sixteen and therefore parental opinions meant little to her, at least on the surface. She laughed. "Whatever. Anyway I did look at those prospectuses you gave me. I'm gonna do a few courses at night, starting September, along with sixth form college."

"Oh, well done! That's great."

She brushed it off, and suddenly brandished a corn dolly under my nose. "Are you doing a scarecrow for the festival?"

"My great aunt is," I said. "It's not suitable for viewing by the under-eighteens, though."

She made an "oooo" of mock indignation.

"Yeah but come on," she insisted. "There's a stall over there where you can make one. Or a corn dolly or something. I wanna see what you come up with."

Lacey had conflicting feelings about me, I knew. She resented me for not teaching her what she perceived to be "real magic" – wiggle your nose and make someone fall in love with you, that kind of thing. But she also knew, and I mean *knew*, on a deeper level, that my magic was a powerful thing and dangerous too. She was fascinated by me and my magical abilities, and a little afraid, which was healthy.

So I humoured her, and as we went across to the busy stall

at the edge of the market, I asked if she had seen Maddie, or Ceri. She shook her head.

"I'll look out for her, though. Here we go, what are you going to make?"

The stall was part of the local community outreach and seemed to be sponsored by all the different groups in Llanfair – the council, the tourist board, the church and the chapel, the schools, and a few local businesses. Everyone was getting behind the scarecrow festival. Locals and visitors alike were being encouraged to make corn dollies, and then bring them along to the festival in a few days' time.

The corn dollies differed in shapes. Some people took it too literally and tried to make doll-shaped things, but in reality, a corn dolly was supposed to be a hoop or plait of twisted straw. There were various suggested patterns laid out on laminated sheets for everyone to ignore.

I wasn't really there to make a corn dolly. I asked everyone if they'd seen Maddie, and described Ceri, but I was disappointed; no one could recall seeing either of them. I even started asking if anyone had seen Owain, but no one had.

I didn't pay much attention to what I was doing. My hands twisted the straw and corn into plaits as I scanned the crowds, seeking Maddie, and also seeking anyone I recognised so that I could ask them if *they* had seen my cousin.

"Ow!" I jerked my fingers in surprise and looked down to see a bright bloom of blood on the yellow straw. Immediately I was beset on all sides by the offer of tissues and sanitising wipes, and the cut to my finger was soon mopped up. The corn dolly itself was stained by the blood.

"How did you do that?" Lacey laughed. "A really sharp bit of straw or something?"

There was no pain at first, like all sharp cuts. I kept a bit of tissue pressed against it, and stuck my tongue out at Lacey. Then a dark head, a few metres away, caught my eye and I called, "Hey!"

But it wasn't Maddie.

"Just call her," Lacey said. "What's the big deal? Borrow my phone."

"Thanks, but you know me and technology. I'll fry it. Anyway, she's out without her phone. I think she might be ill." *No*, I thought to myself. *She's mad about me and the matchmaking. And I was wrong, and I need to apologise. And I need to find Ceri because she's going to be lost, although if she has any sense she will have gone home by now.*

That's where I should go, I realised. *Stop hiding out here and go and face the music. If Ceri and Maddie go anywhere, they'll end up coming home.*

I picked up the half-made corn dolly and shoved it into the baggy side pocket of my cargo shorts. "You know what, I'm going to head home," I said to Lacey. "If you see Maddie, tell her where I've gone."

Lacey shrugged, not wanting to seem to care too much about my movements. I took one last lingering look around at the bustle around me – families with pushchairs, older couples in matching beige, hardy outdoorsy walkers, all the usual throng of a summer in Llanfair – but no Maddie and no Ceri.

I found a burst of enthusiasm from somewhere, and headed first towards Caffi Cwtch. Billy had gone from his place outside, and now two families gathered around the tables. I got almost to the door, intending to pick up some cakes to take back home as a peace offering.

But I got no further.

Gruffydd, the local blacksmith, appeared behind me, and grabbed my arm with unexpected force.

"Bron, so I've found you at last. I felt you were around. Come on."

"Gruffydd!" I was hauled around to face him, but he wasn't smiling in greeting. His sandy hair flopped into his eyes, which were dark and narrowed. Two lines went down his cheeks. He was in an uncharacteristically serious mood. "Hey, what's up?"

"We don't have time. I'll tell you as we go," he said, and actually tugged my arm to get me to start moving. His fingers burned into my skin. "Hurry."

"Where are we going?"

"You are needed at the barrow. *My* barrow," he said.

Five

My questions tumbled out in a stream as we ploughed our way through the crowds and out along a road that soon became a farm track. "What barrow? Do you mean a wheelbarrow? What's injured? What's the urgency?"

His long legs covered the rough ground with more ease than me, so he had more breath with which to reply. "Did you wake up and leave your brain in bed this morning?" he said. "The old barrow up on Penglais. You know where I mean, or you should."

We were heading south, which was the opposite side of town to where I lived, and so it was less familiar territory to me. The track was now nothing more than a path through the heather on the hills and we were still climbing higher and higher. "A prehistoric barrow?"

"Neolithic, yes."

"What do you mean, it's yours?"

He shot me a sideways glance and rolled his eyes slightly. "I am the guardian of it. There always has to be someone, and in this present moment, it has fallen to me."

I learned something new about Gruffydd every time I met

him. Our recent adventures had revealed some dark and powerful magic in him, and it had changed our relationship slightly – sadly, not for the better. I couldn't remember the last time I'd called in at his forge for a cup of tea and a gossip. Now I'd seen him ride at night, and I knew he shoed the horse of the King of Annwn, and he was a dire and fell figure when robed in his power.

It made me nervous, and I didn't like to be nervous. It wasn't that I wanted to be the only witch in the area, but his currents ran deep. And I suppose my biggest problem was that it wasn't entirely clear whether he was on the side of good or evil.

I suspected it was a greyness in between.

Like me.

It didn't comfort me. I knew what sort of person I was, so it was unsettling to think of more like me.

"So what does it mean, you cut the grass around it, that sort of thing?" I said, trying to lighten the mood. "Have open days?"

"I watch the movements around it," he replied. "Both on this plane and … others."

"And is there much movement?"

"Only from Benedict and his ilk."

"Who?"

"Benedict Rigby."

The name tugged at my memory. "He's dead. Long dead. I don't think I ever met him, but I remember seeing him around when I was a kid." He hadn't made any impression on me and he had passed on by the time I was fourteen.

"His little group live on, though, with their mutterings and dark workings. They are mostly harmless, diluted and debased, and of no interest to me."

"Dark workings? They're magical? Was he a witch or a magician or something?"

"He was. And they are, too, in their own ways, but they are to be ignored. Certainly don't you go messing with them. I don't know their motives but they are not likely to be good."

My foot slipped on a rock and he caught me before I even knew I was falling. He set me on my feet again. "Nearly there."

"So what's the issue? An animal, or a bird…?"

He slowed suddenly. "Maddie, of course."

My heart thudded. "What?"

"I thought you knew. You were looking for her, and I have found her. I felt it. Here. There. Look."

Oh, he was an infuriating man. "We're not all mysterious and psychic, you know," I muttered as I looked out across the valley that now spread before us.

The purple heather and yellow-green grass was pocked with grey stones, some as large as a badger, humped and ponderous in the landscape. The hills that dropped away around us mirrored the smaller stones that surrounded the summit in the middle of the bowl that we were approaching. And in the centre of this field of rocks was a strange and artificial grassy lump, with tall grey stones half buried in the earth at one end, and a dark and sinister square between the two pillars.

Rising up out of the sinking depths there was a frantic blonde-haired woman.

It was Ceri, and she launched herself at me with her hands

outstretched, her fingers like talons tipped with shiny red – I thought it was blood for a moment.

How did she get here?

And how on earth had she known to come here?

"That's not Maddie," I said to Gruffydd.

"I know," he replied and there was exasperation in his voice.

"This was your fault!" Ceri screamed, in a high voice, and she jumped at me. Gruffydd stepped in sideways and caught her around her waist before she could make contact. She shrieked and kicked, clawing at me. I stepped back in horror.

"Ceri, calm down! Where's Maddie? Don't worry. We can sort this out." I was feeling a growing terror but I tried not to show it. Her fear was horribly infectious.

She was panting hard and she sagged in Gruffydd's arms, falling against them and flopping like an exhausted child. "She has been taken," she said.

I shivered. But that had happened before and I had dealt with the … the entity … that was responsible. I had no idea what could be going on here. Who or what would take Maddie, and why? "Who, and where?" I demanded, trying to sound controlled and calm.

"She is trapped," Ceri continued. "In there. In the barrow. By him. And I have no power because of…"

"Because of me?" I said. "I don't understand."

"No," she spat. "Not you. It's not all about you, actually, Bron. It's because of *her*."

Six

She was referring to my mother. She *must* have meant my mother. It seemed obvious. But that was a conversation for another time. "Let's get to Maddie," I said confidently. "Who has taken her, where is she, and what do we know about how she is being kept? There are three of us now. We can deal with this."

"It was that little jerk from the barbecue," Ceri said. She struggled weakly in Gruffydd's grasp but it was a half-hearted effort.

"Which one?" I said. There were three. Four, I suppose, if you counted me as a jerk.

"Evan Morley," Gruffydd said. "That's who it is, right? One of Rigby's lot, like I was telling you. He's the worst."

"He was about as magical as a damp towel!" I said in surprise.

"Yeah, well, it's a funny sort of thing," he said, and he didn't mean funny-ha-ha.

I huffed. This was well out of hand. "Right. So, are they in there?"

Gruffydd said, "Wait, we need a plan."

"I have a plan," I said. "I'll get her out and smack that Evan on the nose while I'm at it. Why are you two dithering about?" I strode towards the barrow's entrance. The floor dipped away and led down into a tunnel that was black and chilly. It was much darker than it should have been, as if something within was stealing light. I didn't stop to think, because that would have scared the pants off me. I'd started, all cocky and brave, so I couldn't turn around now. Instead I plunged forward and ducked my head, ready to pass under the stone lintel and enter the barrow.

With a crack and a deep, hollow thumping sound, I was flung backwards out of the barrow's entrance. My heels scrabbled on the rocks and soil and I was lifted up and thrown onto my back, landing about fifteen feet away from the barrow.

Nothing had touched me.

I gasped, winded, and suddenly afraid.

Everyone was silent. My ears were ringing. I hadn't even had time to scream.

Gruffydd let Ceri go, and she stood uncertainly for a moment before coming over to me and saying, with real care, "Are you all right? Oh my god, Bron, what is happening here? Are you okay?"

"No," I said. "What in hell was that?"

"Oh, nothing to do with hell," Gruffydd said. He prowled around the barrow, pacing its length. To one side was a blackened, dead willow tree. He looked at it for a moment, and then came around to the front entrance once more. He peered within, and inhaled.

"Demon traps," he said at last. "Demon traps, laid in the

stone down each side of the passage. You can't see them, but they are there, throbbing. You've excited them."

"That's nonsense," I protested. "I'm not a demon."

"Oh, you don't think?" he said. "You ate the death spirit, remember? There is a demon in you now, whether you like it or not."

"No!" I said, feeling sick. "I'll talk to Horatio…" Could I be exorcised? I'd asked him before but he'd refused. "I don't want a demon inside me."

"It doesn't mean it's an evil one."

"Yes it does," I said. "It's pretty much implied in the name. Demons are evil beings. No one talks about Fluffykins the Sweet Pretty Demon, do they? Oh god, Gruffydd, no…"

"Don't get all worked up about it," Gruffydd said, like it was nothing. He made me feel as if I was making a big fuss about something small like an overdue library book.

And when I glanced at Ceri, I remembered the real reason we were here. She stared at me, and shivered.

But why hadn't Ceri been able to bring her out? "Did they get you too?" I asked.

She wrapped her arms around herself. "No. But I can't get in … I can't go in … it's … she'll know, because she's still here, you see. Please, do something!"

"Why does this Evan even have Maddie in there?" I said, reluctant to approach the barrow again.

"Who cares?" said Ceri. "We have to get her out." And then she pointed at the blackened willow tree. "I did start to go in but … then I heard you all approach. I tried. But she … anyway, she would help *you* if you asked."

The tree was dead, and that made no sense to me. "Gruffydd, did you try to get in? Did the demon traps get you, too?"

"I came straight here as soon as I heard the barrow had been breached," he replied. "I brought you on the way. But they won't get me, no. This place is under my protection. I will go in. I can't feel any other meddling or barriers there. But Bron, you will need to lend me your connections to the land, too. It is an unpredictable magic in there, and alien to us both, I think."

"I thought you were the guardian?"

"Guardians don't control what they guard." He flashed me a sudden grin. "Ask any parent."

"Get. Her. *Out,*" Ceri wailed. "We're wasting time."

She was right. I planted my feet wide apart and drew up the cold, north energy from the earth. I sucked in a breath of pure air, and let it mingle with the fire of my being as the water in my body responded to the throb of the moon.

Ceri went over to the tree, and put her hand on the bark, and stared at me, her face twisted into something between fear and envy as I began my magical working. She was shaking, almost rocking back and forth on the balls of her feet. She seemed pulled and pushed by invisible forces. To go into the barrow; to stay outside of it. Did she know what really lurked within?

My attention was torn from her when Gruffydd touched my shoulders, and inhaled, and nodded. He turned and made for the barrow's entrance. "Look after me, now," he said.

As my senses became heightened, I could hear a chanting,

coming from the immeasurable gloom. "Bring her in. Bring her in," it intoned, in a flat and slightly familiar voice. I thought that it might be Evan.

Who did he want bringing in? Me, Ceri, Maddie? What on earth was happening in there? Panic flared in my belly like a wave of sickness.

Something was happening because as Gruffydd disappeared from view, a roll like thunder came out from the barrow, and Ceri began to cry with loud, gulping sobs, and I forgot all my antagonism with her because she was a mother distraught.

"Get her out, get her out!" Ceri was wailing as the chanting answered, growing louder, "Bring her in, bring her in!"

There was nothing on Ceri's face but pure animal grief and her emotions broke my connection to the land and to Gruffydd. Maddie was in there, and I had to try to get inside again. I couldn't help Gruffydd from outside. I rolled up my power into a ball in my belly and ran right into the barrow.

Whatever the demon traps were, they were invisible to me, as Gruffydd had said, but they punched at me from each side as I slammed into the darkness. I could hear Gruffydd ahead of me, and the chanting of "bring her in" and I found there was still a tiny connection like a sliver of silver between me and him; I blasted back at the dark talons that sought to grab me, and forced my way past the traps.

I was only a little bit demon, I supposed, after all. That was a small comfort, I guess.

But as I congratulated myself about my mostly-humanness, I was slammed from the right side by a force of foetid air that was so foul in stench that it had a physical presence. I lost my footing and went down hard on my left knee. Everything was black and I couldn't see a thing, and my hands touched something soft that wriggled away. I gagged and stumbled as scaly hands came out of the darkness and clawed at my baggy shorts, diving into my pockets and tugging at the hems.

Sickness rose in my throat but Gruffydd called out, then, loud and clear: "I have her! Bron, help me."

Shuddering and flailing my hands, I managed to get back to my feet and ran towards his voice, sending out as much strength as I could spare, imagining a green-white rope of light linking us. And then, ahead of me, I saw a faint glowing and from that glowing came two figures. One was tall and strong, and held the other – a slender female with a mass of hair – and I knew it was Gruffydd and Maddie.

I ran forward, and touched them both, shocking them with a burst of land-energy, and then turned and we plunged into the dark tunnel that would lead us out of the barrow.

Seven

The demon traps helped us this time. Whatever they were, whatever dark magic they used, they were set to expel outwards and so they did; their energy catapulted me back out of the barrow, and Gruffydd and Maddie came behind, breathless. I was launched into the air and I was ready for it this time. I almost laughed but I knew it was a falseness to think that I was using the power. I really had no control. But for a moment, I could fly, in the real world and not just between them.

I landed pretty well, on all fours, and when I turned around there was Gruffydd with Maddie clinging to him. She looked unharmed, but she was blinking in the light and rubbing at her face with her spare arm. There was an air of confusion around her. Her other arm was latched onto Gruffydd and she looked like she wasn't going to let go of the blacksmith for some time.

I caught sight of Ceri out of the corner of my eye but before I could see what she was doing, another person came out of the barrow and he was screaming.

It was Evan Morley, and he was pale, and sweaty, and flinging his arms around. I shouted, "Look out behind you!" but

Gruffydd was already aware of Evan. He pushed Maddie behind him as he faced the furious figure emerging from the barrow.

Evan was not remotely interested in him, nor, strangely, did he head for Maddie. Instead he veered around and made directly for Ceri. "Do you touch her tree? The Unbalancer!" he yelled.

He made no sense to me.

Ceri got herself behind the blackened tree. "Don't you dare come any closer to me."

He paused. His eyes were rimmed with red and he, too, was struggling to see in the sunlight after the darkness of the barrow's interior. He squinted and wiped his mouth with the back of his hand. He stared at us all in turn, and Gruffydd took a step towards him, growling. "What do you think you're playing at? Here, in my barrow?"

Evan couldn't face up to the blacksmith. He fled.

"Go after him," I called, but Gruffydd put out his arm to stop me doing anything rash.

"Let him run. He cannot try anything out here, in the open, not now."

"Maddie, are you hurt?" I asked, as the figure of Evan disappeared over the moors and into a valley.

She looked dazed and confused but there was no sign of blood and my deeper skills as a healer didn't detect anything physically wrong. She shook her head, but then focused on her mother. "Mom!"

Ceri came out from behind the tree but I noticed that she kept one hand on the dead trunk.

"Maddie, oh my god," she said huskily. "Maddie…"

I said, "How did he get you in there?"

She shook her head. "I don't know. I went out to walk off my headache. There was a roaring in my head, you know? I couldn't think straight. I know I should have gone to bed but I just … left. I felt pulled."

"Magic?" I asked, glancing to Gruffydd.

"Yeah, maybe. Or just stress and scotch eggs. Anyway, so I walked, and then … I was here."

"We need to call the police," I said. Ceri nodded.

Maddie put her hands to her face and when she spoke, there was a tremble in her voice. "No, I don't know about that. Mom … mom, what in heck is going on? Evan told me … things. I mean, yeah, I know he was probably lying but I don't know why he would. He said this was because of what you did to aunt Lowri. What did you do? What did you do to your own sister, mom? Why would he say such a thing?"

Ceri shook her head. "No, no, nothing…"

"Mom, what did you do? What is your magic, mom? Is it a dark magic? Is that why you never speak of it?"

I went right up to Maddie's side and put my arm around her but she shook me off angrily. "Maddie, she doesn't have any magic. We know that. You can tell, and I can tell."

She ignored me. "Mom, what did you do?"

"She probably didn't do anything," I said, trying to be a peacemaker, in spite of the twinge in my gut that was saying, actually yeah, she probably did do something because she hadn't been acting normally since she'd arrived. "You know that Evan is a creep and a liar."

"Stop right there!"

And we did. Every single one of us froze as Dilys's voice,

one right from her belly, hardened by years, not a hint of aged tremble in it, nailed us all to the spot. Maybe there was magic in it too, but she didn't need that, when she had decades of survival and grit in her body to call upon.

Even Gruffydd obeyed.

I stood next to Maddie. In front of us was Ceri, touching the tree. Behind us and to one side was Gruffydd.

And around the barrow, coming from the direction of town, was Dilys with a stick in one hand, and Dean the gangly druid hanging on her other arm.

"Do not try to tell me what is going on here," she said, as she came to a halt. She enunciated every syllable with a clipped clearness of a classic Welsh accent. "Do not give me your excuses or your interpretations or your blame. Each of you is wrong, in one way or another. I don't know the truth of it, but nor do any of you. *Any* of you. Now, is anyone hurt? No. Good. We will go home."

She hadn't waited for an answer – she knew none of us were injured.

Maddie opened her mouth and I elbowed her sharply. She scowled at me, but at least she didn't speak.

Dilys turned around, steered by Dean, who towered over her by a good foot or more. We followed, like obedient children.

None of us spoke. I was thinking about the police, and how I should persuade Maddie to speak to them. Maybe I should get Adam to call around.

It was only as we reached the road that would lead us, soon, to our house, that I realised that Gruffydd had not come with us.

Eight

Gruffydd's absence didn't seem to surprise Dilys but the man was raising more and more questions in my head.

Not as many as the whole Ceri-Maddie-Lowri thing, though. Ceri, especially. I promised myself I would not jump to any conclusions. Emotions were running high and we needed to be calm about this. We took our places around the messy kitchen table. No one went to put the kettle on. Dean excused himself, and Dilys sent him away with her thanks and a fruit pie. Now, just the four of us were left. One family, riven by historical and geographical divisions.

Ceri was crying, very quietly, just tears rolling down her face. Maddie sat opposite to her, and she had a blank expression on her face. I wondered again if she'd been stunned, or magically bound in some way. I probed gently but there was no trace of it now. The Fair Folk were coming to her aid, and I felt a flutter of silver wings brush against me.

I said, "Ceri, although I don't trust Evan and don't think he's telling the truth, I know there is something in the past that you need to share. Please, tell me what you did to my mother."

Ceri patted at her eyes for a moment. I pushed a roll of thick kitchen paper across to her. She looked at it with distaste but pulled a sheet free and mopped up her tears. She linked her fingers together, moving them constantly in a dance of anxiety. I didn't ask her again. I could see that she was sorting out her thoughts.

What she said then was completely unexpected.

"I am so sorry. I had to bind her power into the willow tree by the barrow."

I said, "What?" at the same time as everyone else, our questions chorusing together – even Dilys, and that made me realise that she had been telling the truth when she'd said she didn't know everything.

"I had power once," Ceri went on. "I did. But I gave it all up. I had to."

"You used your power all up, just to bind my mother's own power?" I asked. "Why? There had to be a reason why. That's not something anyone just … does."

"I grew up as an only child," Ceri said. "Lowri had left home by the time I was five years old. I didn't see her much. She never wanted a kid hanging around; who would, right? Now when I got to sixteen myself, I could feel this … power, I guess … rising in me. Lowri was about thirty by this time."

"Before she had me, though," I said.

"Sure, right. I didn't know what was happening and so I went to talk with her. You know, big sister wisdom and all. I knew she had power herself. I thought she might reassure me. And so she took me to see one of her friends. This guy, well, this creep, called Benedict Rigby."

That name again. Gruffydd had mentioned him. And he was dead now. Oh god, was I going to have to hedge ride to sort this out?

She continued. "I believed everything that he told me and everything he told her. Of course I did. I shouldn't have. She believed him too, and I trusted her. And I don't think there was a scrap of evil in your mom, Bron. No, not ever. But she was led astray by that man. I started to realise something was wrong in my dreams, when they changed. There was a polecat, he'd come to me, and I promised that I would help, but I didn't know what I was doing, or why. What was real? At night, only the dreams were real."

"And what was happening during the day?" I asked.

Ceri bowed her head. "I didn't really realise it then, but they were drawing away my power. I couldn't control it. They used me. I know that Lowri wanted children, more than anything else … oh Bron. I don't mean to say but … that's what she wanted and she would do anything for it. For you."

"No, no," I said, my head spinning. *No. Not this, not for me.* I couldn't hold the indirect blame. Dilys reached out her wrinkled hand and patted mine.

"Shush," she said.

"I had to stop it all happening, I had to. For me, and also for Lowri. She was never evil, Bron, but she was under their sway and things were going to go so wrong. My dreams told me so. The polecat guided me."

"You did what you had to do," I said slowly, trying to make

my feelings fit my words.

"I am so ashamed," Ceri said.

I didn't understand. "What for?"

"For everything that happened and went wrong. It shouldn't have gone the way that it did. I was left with no magic, and so was your mom; hers was all tied up in that tree, in the end."

The tree was dead now. But so was my mother. That fitted together. And it explained some of Ceri's words, and why she kept on touching the tree by the barrow. I shivered. So my mam's old power was still in it?

I probed but there was no hint of duplicity in Ceri's words. I looked across to Maddie, and said, quite rudely I know, "Is she lying?"

Maddie must have been asking herself the same thing. She had her eyes half-closed, hunting for the cracks in the dialogue, and she said, very quietly, "No. She is telling the truth."

Dilys gave my hand a squeeze and I got violently to my feet. The chair legs scraped on the tiled floor. I couldn't say anything else. My head was whirling and I felt ill.

"I need some air. Sorry – excuse me."

I went out to my willow cave in the garden, and curled up there, in the safest place I had ever really known.

***

I would like to say that I wasn't having a bit of a dramatic moping moment but we all know that would be a lie. I am only human, the small demon-part of me notwithstanding. I was feeling confused and upset, but instead of being an adult and staying to talk about it with the people closest to me, I went outside to hide, but made sure that everyone *knew* I was going outside to hide. And if you think that's childish of me, you're totally right.

You would have done the same. At least for a little while.

Anyway, I did need to get a few things straight in my head. Harkin padded out to join me. At least it was a nice warm day. It would have suited my melancholic and melodramatic mood a little more if it had been cold and raining but you can't have everything. I leaned back against the rough bark of the hawthorn. The tree and the willow around me was in the full livery of summer, and I was hidden from view by a mass of green. I inhaled deeply and let the warm, sultry air and cloying pollen fill my lungs. I was out of the hot sun, and the ground beneath me was cool.

I believed Ceri. She had no magic in her now, at any rate. I could well imagine that as a girl, she had power – it was our heritage. As for my mother, she had died before I had understood what magic was, so I had no memory of whether she had had power or not.

And my mother had been allied to Benedict Rigby. No one had contradicted that.

And Benedict Rigby had been a magician. That I also believed.

And my mother had tried to take the power from her sister, my aunt – Ceri.

Could I believe that?

I had to.

I breathed in and out, and the tree behind me breathed also. That reminded me of the matter of the trees – the two trees. The blackened, dead willow by the barrow had held my mother's power out of her reach.

But what of the tree that Billy had reminded me of? Ceri's Tree, as we all called it. The silver birch. Ceri herself had not mentioned that in her most recent explanation.

What about the polecat? I wasn't sure. I hadn't seen any around for a long while.

And why, of all things, was *Maddie* now a target? Ceri's return had triggered something. Maddie had not been a target for them before. So, why now?

Evan Morley had taken her, or so it seemed. Would he come for her again? Maddie didn't want police involvement and seemed confused as to what had happened. I needed to talk to her about that, and see if her memories could be jogged. It was important. Had she been forcibly taken, or not?

I could sulk out here in the cave all day, but meanwhile, my cousin was still – potentially – in danger. If only I knew Evan's motives. It would make him easier to stop, I thought.

As if drawn outside by my musings about her, Maddie appeared in the gap between the land and sky, and she had a cup of tea in her hand.

She crouched briefly, and placed it on a flat patch of baked earth, and retreated out of sight, hidden by the foliage within moments. I heard the back door close.

My throat ached with rawness. She, too, had faced

unpleasant revelations, but she wasn't lurking in a hedge about it. I wanted to call her back.

I touched my fingertips to the hot mug as if the sharp pain would recall me to myself, and my mission.

Yes. *Yes.* I had things to do.

Where did this evil really come from? Was it not, in fact, something that dwelled within the barrow? It could have infected Benedict Rigby and his more recent followers, Evan and Owain and John; it could have made victims of them all, and Ceri and Lowri too.

But Gruffydd was the guardian of the barrow.

I picked up the cup and sipped at the tea.

Was Evan a bad person?

Was my mother?

What did it even mean?

NINE

I wasn't going to hedge ride right now, that was for sure. Maddie was in danger in the real world, right now. Evan had taken her – but was he really the dangerous one, or was he acting under the influence of something, or someone, else? All this had been triggered by the arrival of Ceri, it seemed.

But why did they want Maddie, what would they do … and why had they only acted now?

I drained the cup and left it there in the willow cave. I didn't go back inside the house, not yet. I'd leave Ceri to recover a little more from her jetlag, and Maddie to relax after her ordeal. I hoped that Dilys was subtly probing for answers, then I caught that thought. Dilys and subtle?

I skirted around the edge of the house, bid Harkin goodbye, and set out in search of answers.

I set out to talk to John Morgan Driscoll.

***

I knew where I'd find him. He lived in a semi-detached house on an old post-war housing estate that had once been on the edge of town, but now the grey pebble-dashed houses were hemmed around with newer buildings, all built in red brick with tiny gardens. John's house, though, was square and blocky and had large grounds to three sides of it. It was strange how the larger houses were the older, and cheaper, ones.

His neighbours were poor, and often out of work. The mother spent her time cleaning everything, because appearances still mattered, to her. The father was sitting on a chair on the front lawn when I went up the straight grey path to John's house, and he called a greeting over the low clipped privet hedge that divided the two front gardens.

"He'll be around the back, love," he said. "Do you want a beer?"

"No, thank you. You keeping well?"

"Can't complain. Send my regards to your aunt." He meant Dilys, of course, not Ceri.

I didn't bother to knock on John's door. I followed the path down the side of the house and came out to the mess of timber buildings and wire mesh that was John's back yard.

The aviaries and bird cages had grown over the years, with lean-tos and additions sprouting like crystals blooming, a fractalling of shades of brown. John himself was standing in a narrow walkway between two eight-foot-high enclosures, and measuring something from a bottle into a syringe. He flicked his head as I approached, so he knew that I was there, but he continued with his task, drawing up some liquid into the needle.

When he was done, he looked up.

"Bron. Got a bird for me?"

He was never one for small talk. To my right, a red kite began to call, a piercing whistle.

"No, I haven't," I said. I faced him as boldly as I could. He was bigger than me, and wiry like leather ropes. His eyes were so pale as to be reflections of the summer sky. "I want to know what happened today, at the barrow. And I want to know what happened years ago, with Benedict Rigby. And I want to know what sort of magic you lot are up to, and why Maddie is the target."

I watched his face as carefully as one of his hawks but he didn't betray a single thing by any twitch or movement.

That was suspicious in itself, I thought. *Too much of a poker face, then.*

But he said, off-hand and casually, "I have no idea what happened at the barrow today. Why don't you tell me, eh?"

"Evan Morley was there. And he is one of you."

"What Evan does is up to him."

"You're friends."

"I don't really do friends. Never have. Complicated. I have birds. Much easier." He spoke in short bursts like conversation was unwelcome to him, and he only rarely met my eyes. Most of his attention was focused on the birds around him.

"You release them all eventually, don't you?" I said.

"Of course. What use is a bird in a cage?"

While we both regarded the kite who was still calling, I probed him for any sign of magical ability or power.

And there *was* something.

I hadn't noticed it before, partly because I don't really go around looking for it – sometimes it's easier not to know. And I shield myself a lot from the world outside, so as not to blow up random electronics as I pass. It's not a one-way shield. If I cut myself off from influencing things, then also things can't get in to influence me. I miss out on obvious things, sometimes. Like, yeah yeah, tact and human decency – I know!

I tried to feel out what sort of magic he contained but it was buried deep. He turned to look at me, and his ice-like eyes made me shiver.

"You're looking, aren't you?" he said, and I knew that he knew. "You're in my head."

I withdrew my attention.

"You can hardly blame me," I said.

That made him grin. "I've always liked you, Bronwen Talog. We all have, haven't we?"

I hadn't noticed the arrival of Owain and Evan. As soon as I saw Evan all the hairs went up along my back and arms. He smiled toothily at me, and I wanted to punch him. He looked a bit better than when he had fled the barrow. I supposed that he felt safer with company around him. I clenched my fists briefly.

"Yeah, we like you very much, Bron," Evan said slimily.

"I do not like you – what the hell was that stunt you pulled at the barrow? I ought to phone the police on you. In fact I bet that Maddie already has." I hoped she had. I would drag her to the station myself.

"She hasn't, and she won't, you know. I didn't harm her

and anyway, I was always going to let her go. She walked with me of her own free will."

"She would not have done that. It was still kidnapping."

He shrugged, an infuriating reply of indifference. "Nah. She walked with me and Owain in town and then we went there."

Oh. If Owain had been there, she might have gone along with it. But she hadn't mentioned him.

"What about those demon traps around the barrow?" I went on. "And why did you take her, or walk with her, or whatever it is you are claiming that you did, anyway?" I tried to fix each of them in turn with my glare, like I was an angry school teacher telling her pupils off. But they laughed at me.

I could feel my anger pulling my power into a small, tight ball in the centre of my stomach. I took a few deep breaths.

John cocked his head at Evan. "I don't really know what you were up to, mate," he said. "Go on, then. Tell us. Demon traps? Really?" He laughed.

That was a surprise to me. I thought the three of them were in cahoots. Evan said, "That was a lucky accident, really. I didn't set them. I didn't even know they were there till that blacksmith started going on about them. They must have been there from way back to protect the barrow. I couldn't see anything so I reckon they were just carvings in the rock or something."

Then he grinned at me. "But they got you, didn't they? Demon! Ha. So what was all that about? What's inside you? You a necromancer or something? Wow."

"I am not going to tell you a thing," I retorted. "Why did you take Maddie?"

Evan looked at John and Owain, and chortled. "Oh, she's so angry! Bron, don't you know that we wouldn't want any harm to come to you? Never, not you."

"What about Maddie?"

Evan continued to evade my question. "We're protecting you, you know. It's about you. We've always looked out for you. It's in our book, you see."

"What about Maddie?" I could hear my voice rising.

But it was like shouting at a cliff face. They steadfastly refused to answer my one simple question, and I felt sure it was a power play by them. They were mocking me and it was making me more and more angry. I had to keep a lid on it, or they would easily push me to explode. I could not afford to lose control.

"You're mentioned in the Book of Dooms, you know," Evan carried on.

John put out a hand, just a quick twitch, and let it drop. He didn't speak to him, but I saw his expression. He was warning Evan.

"We're done here, Bron," John said. "Ignore this pair of jokers. Sorry about Maddie and all that. I am sure it won't happen again, will it?"

Evan said, "I solemnly promise not to take Maddie to the barrow again."

"That is not what he meant," I said. "If you so much as come near her, or me, or any of us again, I will phone the police."

"But you won't. You won't have any reason to. Your big strong policeman boyfriend can stay in his box, so don't you worry," Evan said. "You have always been ours. You're one of us, you know. Demon traps got you! That is great. You can really work with that."

"Time to go," John said. He moved towards me as if he was going to take my elbow and steer me out. I shot out a dozen invisible psychic spikes around me and he stopped, detecting them.

"I am going," I said. "You three are idiots. Playing stupid mind games and talking total shit. I'm not into it. I don't know your game but you leave us all alone. You too, Owain. Maddie doesn't want to see you any more."

Owain hadn't said a thing during the whole exchange. If anything, he looked supremely uncomfortable. He met my eyes and he was trying to say something, but I had not time for that.

"We're helping you, Bron. You watch out, now. Watch your back. She's The Unbalancer," Evan said.

"Maddie?"

"No, that woman."

"Ceri?" I asked, and thought, *or do you mean my mam, or whatever is left of her in that tree?*

"You know," Evan said. "You know who I am talking about. You'll come back to us. It's in the blood, Bronwen Talog."

They were around me in a semi-circle. I felt Evan pulling me towards him and John trying to push me away.

Owain remained silent. He didn't even look at me now. He was backing away. He was on the edge of things and I thought he didn't really want to be a part of it, now that he could see what Evan was really like.

I fled, walking briskly in a not-quite-a-run way, but my pace got quicker and quicker as I went and by the time I was a hundred yards down the road, I was jogging, and I did not look back.

***

My thoughts, as I left the housing estate, circled around one very important and potentially impossible thing: *How did you make a truth serum?*

That was what bugged me the most. I'd asked questions and they hadn't answered them. They obviously didn't want me to know, but it was also because they wanted to mess with me. I hated it.

Okay, I was saying 'they' but I meant Evan. Owain was trying to extricate himself from them, and John was – exactly as he had said – not concerned with friends or connections. He was guilty by association, though.

Evan. He was the one. I wanted to wipe his smug mocking smile off his face. He was noticeably more confident when he wasn't alone.

So, how was it possible to force someone to tell the truth? I didn't do traditional spell craft particularly – you know, the whole chant a poem thing, while candles of special colours burned and you threw carefully chosen essential oils around. But in this case, I was prepared to have a go. There had to be a spell to make someone speak the truth. Maybe I could concoct some kind of food and trick them into eating it. Or inject a truth serum into a cheap can of lager, as that seemed to be Evan's thing.

I decided to take a wander. The day was drawing to a close

now; the kerfuffle at the barbecue seemed a long time ago, though it had only been a few hours. Still, summer days were long and I had many hours of warm daylight left. I knew I had to get home and speak properly to Maddie, and I felt sure I should talk to Adam.

But first, I wanted to check something else out.

I headed out to the commons, and towards Ceri's Tree. I wanted to find out more about this overlooked yet familiar landmark. How long did a silver birch tree live for? Twenty years, domestically, maybe more? It could have been a sapling when Ceri last lived her. Did she plant it herself?

If I did make a working truth drug, I might as well just unleash it on everyone, in one big session, and get everything over and done with – bam, all sorted. I liked that idea.

Okay, so there were some minor issues of consent and all that, but as far as I was concerned, Evan had forfeited any rights to that when he took Maddie.

She definitely needed to call the police about it.

Then I slowed my pace. I was on the grassland now, and alone. Why hadn't Gruffydd phoned the police? Instead he'd come to me. But surely any normal human's instinct would be to call the authorities.

I hadn't, either, but I don't claim to be normal. I had been caught up in the panic of the moment. In hindsight, it was reckless, and I needed to ask some stern questions about Gruffydd.

I imagined trying to explain myself to Adam and I cringed. He was already not happy with me.

I put that out of my mind as I got to the tree. The silver birch was tall and although the trunk was straight, it leaned at an angle due to the years of prevailing winds. The leaves shimmered and danced in the lightest of breezes. It stood alone, like it was a slightly aloof person at a party – there were other stands of trees around, but they clustered together in little cliques.

The ground immediately under the tree was bare earth, ivy and nettles. I put my hands on the flaking bark and looked up into the muddle of branches and twigs. Even in the height of summer, it wasn't densely packed with foliage and I saw blue sky between the twisting leaves.

The tree itself didn't feel any different to how I expected it to feel. Light green lines of slow-moving sap-like energy flowed up and down and it was surrounded by a golden-brown glow which plunged deep into the earth, and I could feel the lines of the roots spreading out as far as the branches above reached.

I closed my eyes and inhaled, and held my breath. I would have to hedge ride to get much more information, however, and I wouldn't be able to get anything directly from the tree itself. My best chance was to commune with the spirits of place around the tree and hope that they were disposed to help me.

"Hoom, hoom, hoom!" came a low, booming voice, and I swallowed an involuntary squeak.

Maddie appeared, walking stiff-legged and rolling from side to side. "Hoom, hoom, hoom!"

"Are you trying to be an Ent?" I asked. Tolkien was one of my favourite authors.

"Hey, well done!"

"You're moving too fast for Treebeard."

"But apart from that, I was pretty convincing, right?"

She smiled and I smiled back, one of those tentative exchanges that two people do after they parted on uncertain emotional terms. We checked each other's faces for confirmation that everything was going to be okay.

I think that it was.

She said, suddenly awkward, "Hey. You all right?"

"Of course I am. And you?"

"Yeah, sure. I mean, it's not like anything traumatic has happened, you know?"

"Exactly. Worse things happen at sea and all that. Maddie, do you have any idea why he took you? Have you remembered anything yet?"

"Not a clue. He said some pretty strange things to me but you know, I think he's just mad."

"No, don't excuse his actions," I said. "He knew right from wrong. Mad, maybe, but also bad. Um, was Owain with him when you met him in town?"

She screwed up her face. "It's hazy. I had this headache, because I hadn't been sleeping and all. So when it all happened, I just wanted to get away from the smoke and the noise. And I was only outside the house, really, when Owain and Evan came up to me." She spoke slowly. "Oh, it's kinda coming back to me as I talk. Okay, so I wanted to be on my own. I didn't actually mean to go anywhere, I think … but I wanted to be away from them. They were coming from the garden and I didn't want to go past them. Does that sound stupid?"

"Not at all. I wouldn't want to be within twenty metres of Evan."

"Right, sure. So, I walked the other way and they followed. Actually Owain talked to me and I liked that. But Evan came along too, like a third wheel, and then he was doing all the talking and I was trying to blot him out, and my head was pounding, and Evan told Owain to go get me a bottle of water from a shop, and I felt faint."

"And then what?"

She looked at me with misery on her face. "I can't remember a thing. Did I faint? Did Owain come back? Did Evan charm me? Did I willingly go with him? The next thing I am sure of was being in the barrow, but I didn't know that was where I was. And Evan was telling me stuff about how … how my mom was … evil."

"She is not, and we know he is a liar," I told her firmly.

"Do you think he'll come after me again?" she asked. "I kinda sneaked away from the house, you know. My mom needed calming down so Dilys made her something which smelled … questionable. I didn't want to drink it. And while they were settling down in the living room, I came out for a walk. I know, I know! After all that happened! But this time I wrapped myself in my Faerie glamour. They're with me."

I nodded. I could feel them.

She went on, saying, "Oh – yeah, I left them a note too, don't worry. They won't think it's happened again, and panic."

I let out a sigh of relief. "I don't think that Evan will come after you," I said, but I wasn't so sure, in truth. He had only promised not to take her to the barrow, after all. And what was his promise worth?

If I said that I thought Maddie and her mother were in danger, they would leave. They'd be on the next flight to America. For all I knew, Ceri was booking the return trip right at this moment.

I didn't want them to be in danger, but I didn't want them to leave.

Anyway, that wouldn't solve the mystery of *why* Evan wanted her, and what all the guff about my own mother was about.

"Maddie, about my mam…"

She linked her arm into mine. "I can't imagine what you're feeling right now," she said, but I felt a warmth emanate from her as she soothed me with her Faerie glamour. I would usually shake it off, but this time I accepted it. "But whatever they say, she was your mom and she loved you very much." She reassured me just as I had done for her.

She couldn't know that for sure. My mam, by all accounts, had been allied to some very dodgy people indeed. I wasn't about to say that I was the daughter of an evil witch.

But it was a thought that I was struggling with.

"Come on," she went on. "Let's go home. It's been a long day."

"Maddie, we should speak to the police. Or at least Adam."

She tossed her head. "You should speak to Adam, yeah," she said.

I knew what she meant. And I would get around to it. Soon.

TEN

Ceri descended on Maddie as soon as we re-entered the kitchen. Whatever herbal draught that Dilys had inflicted on her made Ceri's movements slow and dull. She grabbed her daughter and squeezed her tightly. "How was I supposed to know that the note wasn't fake?" she said, muffled by Maddie's shoulder. "Don't you do that again, you hear? After everything that's happened … oh my god, Maddie, we were about to call 911."

"999," she said. "Hey, I just went for a walk."

"That's what you did last time. How could we know?"

That was a fair point.

Ceri towed Maddie into the snug, under-used living room and I squared up to my aunt. She settled herself down on a chair with a sigh, and said, "You are about to have a go at me, aren't you?"

I leaned back against the rail at the front of the Aga. Even in the heat of August, the range kept on burning. It wasn't like a domestic gas or electric oven, turned on and off at the flick of a switch. It had to be kept lit so that it was ready to cook or provide hot water whenever we needed it.

"Not exactly," I said. "First of all, do you know any spells that would make someone tell the truth?"

She pursed her wrinkled lips. "I am hurt, I am. For shame! I will always tell you the truth, Bron."

"I know that. I didn't mean for me to use on you. I went to see John and those other two turned up – Evan and Owain – and they wouldn't answer my questions. They're playing games with me. Also … what do you think about Gruffydd?"

"What about him?" Her dark, sparse eyebrows shot up. "You cannot suspect him of anything but good intentions and good purpose."

"There is something he's not telling me, I am sure of it."

"No doubt, but that would only be because you didn't need to know it."

"I'll decide that. Seriously, aunt, how can I make people tell the truth?"

She sucked her teeth. "Do you think it's right or ethical to do that?"

"That hardly matters when someone's life is in danger."

She didn't reply.

She didn't need to.

I listened to my words again, in my head.

I sighed. "Okay then. Let me tell you what those men just told me, and see what you think about it all then."

She nodded. "Best get the kettle on, then."

I brewed up, and as I worked around the kitchen, making tea and tidying up at the same time, I explained what I'd learned earlier. I watched her as closely as I could, too, trying to detect from her facial expressions what she already knew.

I was getting paranoid. I was starting to think that everyone around me was lying to me.

There wasn't a lot to tell, and I put the cups of tea on the table and sat down as I got to the end of everything. "So there you are," I said. "Ceri was right. My mam was involved with those clowns. They've got some kind of book, they're dark magicians; and they seem to want to get hold of Maddie but won't tell me why, nor why they acted now, and whether Ceri is anything to do with it. She's definitely not magical," I added. "Not any more, at any rate."

Dilys tapped her brittle nails on the cup. "Things are falling into place," she admitted.

"Did you really not know any of this?"

"I'd been away. I was travelling a lot. But I knew of that Benedict Rigby. He was an older man, but very suave, very dashing. Everyone fancied him, if I tell the truth. They really did! I think we all knew he was a wrong one but still, he had that way of talking to you like you were the most important person on earth at that moment."

"He sounds like a creep."

"He was a sexy, good-looking, attentive, polite creep then," Dilys said. "He charmed everyone, both men and women, and you could forgive him anything. Don't blame your mam for falling under his spell."

"But she had power of her own. She was an adult. A grown woman who could make her own choices," I argued. "I actually find it easier to forgive Ceri because she was only a teenager and she didn't know what was happening to her."

"The thing about being an adult," Dilys said, "is that it really turns out to be no different to being a child or a teenager. You're an adult. But you're hardly perfect. How old do you feel, inside?"

"I don't know. Twenty-two, twenty-three?"

"Poppycock. Half the time you're sixteen and so is everyone else. Yes, even me. A switch doesn't flip when you get past twenty, you know. You don't suddenly get sensible and rational. Benedict Rigby made your mam feel like she was a giggling teenager again, you mark my words."

"Right, okay. So what do we do now? Because honestly, Dilys, I think that Maddie might still be in danger. They are up to something, those three."

"Definitely all three?"

"Okay, definitely Evan. John seems to know things; he won't get involved but he watches from the side. He is guilty because of his lack of action, you know. As for Owain, he looks like he's along for the ride but he seems a bit clueless. I think he wants out of it. So it's mostly Evan."

"Maddie has power," Dilys said. "I wonder if that's what they want? But Ceri can't protect her. Her own power, the Faerie stuff, isn't going to be an adequate protection. So we must do it."

"Yes," I said, "but that's not enough. I won't just hem her round with protection and wait to be attacked. We did that before, remember, with Dean. It didn't go well. No, we need to be active. We're not going to be victims. She won't be safe until we have *got rid of Evan Morley*." I punched the table with each word. "I will *act.*"

Dilys took a long, slow and noisy drink of her tea. She replaced the cup carefully and narrowed her eyes. I knew what she was going to say. "What do you mean by 'got rid', Bron? How are you going to act? Are you talking of a banishing, then?"

"Perhaps."

"You would truly become your mother's daughter?"

That stung. I winced. "No. My intentions are good."

"Well, perhaps your mam thought that too."

"I'll never know, will I?" I said bitterly.

She snorted with laughter. "You what now?"

I opened my mouth to repeat myself, but my aunt was not deaf.

Then the penny dropped. I sat back and thought about it. It was possible.

"Okay then. I'll hedge ride"

"When?"

"Tonight."

Dilys laughed. "After the day we've had?"

"We can't afford to wait. I will find her, and I will ask her." And unlike people still stuck in their corporeal bodies, spirits and shades could not lie. There was no need of a truth drug when you journeyed beyond the veil.

"But Dilys," I went on, as fear gnawed at me again. "Dilys, what if I find out something that I don't like?"

She didn't laugh any longer. She said, "What could be worse than what you already know?"

Eleven

I had barely eaten all day, not since the truncated midday barbecue, and when it came to the delayed and very late evening meal, I only picked at that, too. I knew I could stand to lose a few pounds, and journeying on an empty belly was better, anyway. There was plenty of quick food in the fridge waiting for me on my return.

I didn't tell Maddie or Ceri what I was intending to do, but I didn't need to. Maddie knew my rituals and I supposed that someone would fill Ceri in on what I was doing. She had gone to bed early, jetlagged and exhausted.

Dilys watched me carefully.

No one spoke much. I think we were all worn out and exhausted. It wasn't the best decision to go journeying in such a state, but I felt that I didn't want to waste any time.

"You should eat more," Maddie said as I stood up and began to gather the plates.

"I'm not hungry."

"Are you okay? I mean, like, really okay?"

I was saved from answering by a rap at the back door, and

the arrival of Adam. He was in his uniform. After the barbecue he'd gone off to do a shift as a police officer. He held his hat in his hands, and apologised for interrupting us all so late.

"Maddie! Thank heavens."

"Hey, Adam."

He came into the kitchen and grinned with sheer relief. "You guys all disappeared and told me to look after Dilys."

She snorted.

"I know, I know, you don't need looking after. Nor did you need me to tidy up the kitchen, make you a brew quickly followed by a hot toddy, and empty the cat litter tray."

She simply smiled smugly.

"Anyway," Adam continued, "you know I had to go to work, but why didn't you call me to tell me that Maddie was back?"

"Sorry. I didn't think," I said.

"I asked.

"Ah. I heard you shout something as I left but I didn't hear what it was."

His happiness at finding Maddie safe and well was beginning to evaporate. "So you didn't stop to ask me to repeat it?"

"I was in a hurry," I said. "Look, sorry, okay? We're all tired. And she's fine. But…"

I gave her a hard stare. She shook her head very slightly. So, she wasn't going to tell him what had happened, then. That was infuriating, but that was her decision.

"What?" Adam asked. "What are you two not telling me? Dilys, you will be honest with me."

"See," Dilys said to me, "you don't need to make a truth drug."

Adam nearly exploded. "What?"

"Thanks, aunt," I muttered. To Adam, I said, "Ignore her. She's old and batty."

"That's rude," Adam said, and Dilys grinned at me from behind his back.

I rolled my eyes. But I didn't get to unleash any smart retort because then someone else came in and this person didn't even knock.

It was Gruffydd.

He nodded brusquely at everyone, and lingered particularly on Maddie. "Evening, all. I just wanted to see how you were, Maddie," he said.

Adam folded his arms. I didn't understand why Adam and Gruffydd didn't get on, but that was their business. Maddie, sensitive to these things, fluttered her eyes for a moment and I detected a tingle of glamour as she sought to soothe over any potential snide that could happen. But she was tired, too, and her Faerie magic was weak at the moment.

"I'm fine, thank you," she said. "I'm just off to bed."

"Ah, yeah, sorry; I shouldn't have come around so late," Gruffydd said, and Adam frowned in agreement, as if he, too, wasn't doing exactly the same thing. "It's just after everything, you know, I thought it best to check. But I don't think you have anything to fear now. I've spoken to John Driscoll and he says he doesn't know why Evan is like he is, but it's not anything that their group have organised or condone, and John's going to talk to Evan."

Adam said, "What are you talking about? Organised, condoned, what?"

Maddie stood up and faced them both, trying to smile with a relaxed manner. "Hey, guys, so I really appreciate everyone's concern and all, but it's been a real long day and I'm beat, you know? Gruffydd, thank you for coming out to help look for me. Adam, I ended up getting kinda lost, and Gruffydd was there to help out. The thing with Evan … he was joshing with me, trying to kid around. Um. Well, that's mostly it. Okay, so goodnight, all!"

She picked up a glass of water from the table and dashed off. Adam glared at me. "She got lost? She's been here months."

I had to say something. "There's a bit more to it than that, and I will try to get her to tell you everything. But she's had such a rough day."

"Can't you tell me?"

"It's up to her. I'm sorry."

Adam looked at Dilys, and Gruffydd. "Everyone else knows."

"It's up to Maddie!" I repeated.

He looked hurt. But he didn't say anything about loyalties, or being excluded, or priorities. He was too much of a gentleman. "I don't deserve you," I said, out of nowhere.

He looked at me strangely. "No, you don't. Good night, everyone."

He left, and after a moment, without a word, so did Gruffydd.

Dilys tutted at me. "Haven't you got things to be getting on with?"

"Huh."

I left her to the tidying up. I'd cooked, after all, though I suspected I would still have the washing-up to do in the morning. I went upstairs and I took a bath, lingering in the water, letting my mind empty both of mundane thoughts – blue bubble bath or yellow? – and the more serious issues. Maddie, Ceri, and Adam. And Evan.

Harkin stayed at my side, in a nest of towels on the chair. Then he plodded out with me to the willow cave as the late dusk finally passed into night. The sky remained light very late at this time of year, but it was not as warm as you might expect, especially when you're sitting on the ground. I wrapped myself in my particular cloak, and lit a small fire between myself and the outside world. I had my stang, which was a forked stick, reminiscent of a witch's broom which would be ridden between the worlds, and I had my secret mask which no one else except me had ever seen.

My belly rumbled and it was partly its emptiness and partly nervousness. One of the really big and important parts of being a hedge witch was basically *not* really hedge riding very much. Not all hedge witches ride the hedge; it's a term that can mean different things to different people. But I resisted the label of 'shaman' which others tried to put on me, because that was a wholly different cultural thing as far as I was concerned.

However, just about every culture, as far as I could tell, had some kind of tradition for people like me – people who would mediate between the living and the dead, and hunt for answers not in the Underworld but certainly in the Otherworld and along the edges of our perceptions and existences. I did like the term 'soul midwife'.

I focused on the flames which were dancing and as I stared, they seemed to grow still. They expanded in my vision until yellow and orange was all that I could see. They died down to a glowing ember and I shrank with them, folding in on myself, sliding down the tree roots into the dank cold earth itself, into the depths of the soil that never grew warm from month to month to year to year.

The world shifted suddenly ninety degrees and I was not sinking into the earth at all, but flying high in the sky. There were no clouds and the air was chill up here, and the far horizons were tinged grey as the sun still had her influence.

I flew and I was almost a bird but I was not a bird. It was as if an image of a bird was superimposed upon me. I flew, my shoulders aching already, my breath hammered back into my throat and making me gasp with the effort of breathing. But I did not fly – I was carried. But I was not passive – I was active. To fly and to not fly. In the spaces between those two polarities, that was where I existed.

These things are not understood in words.

I was not alone. She flew with me. She was like a raven, usually, but that was just an easy form for Her to assume that I could understand with my feeble, earth-bound human brain. We do like to label things, and the label makes a boundary and the boundary becomes a chain, and therein begins so many problems.

But let us call Her a raven, for now.

She knew my purpose and She flew with me, guiding me across the night town, sleepy but not fully asleep. Cars wove up and down the streets, their presence announced by the reflections of their headlights on other things. Some things you only ever know by the impression that they leave behind.

The town fell away and now we headed south. I realised that we were going towards the barrow, and I would have hesitated, but this was an important task.

Also, if you hesitate when you're flying, you plummet to the ground, so there's that.

The barrow was hard to see from above, and there was only a quarter moon which did not cast much shadow. I recognised it from the dead willow, and in this place between the worlds, the tree itself seemed to be glowing.

I landed lightly on the grass. First I looked at the barrow, and it seemed to look back at me. I circled it, and did not approach the entrance. I knew that in this realm, the barrow's tunnel could lead to some strange and dark places indeed.

The tree seemed to give off a pale grey light. It was dead, but here it seemed to still harbour something.

I was here to find my mother's shade and speak with her.

When I remembered that, a cold sweat drenched me. In spite of having lost her so young, and in spite of my own abilities and talents, I had never even once thought of seeking her spirit out. It was never a task I would do lightly, anyway. I had had counselling, as a child, and I was lucky to have done so. She had died of illness, no tragic accident, and school and the community had supported me well, and great aunt Dilys had stepped up to the bar when my father also, suddenly, passed away. I had never felt truly alone, though I had had passing lonelinesses. When the magic came for me, it filled in some of the gaps, and I learned to live with the spaces in my life and my memory where others would have had a mother.

So it felt strange to be standing here in search of something that I had learned to live without. Unhealthy, almost.

The tree shivered and it seemed as if the few remaining stubby branches rubbed against one another. They creaked like the laughter of old men.

The raven had left me.

I felt sure that She would still be near if I needed Her, but this was something I was clearly supposed to do alone.

I approached the tree.

The glowing increased as I got closer, and when I was five feet away from it, the branches nearest to me suddenly dipped and probed towards me like hands. I stepped back hastily, just out of reach, and the tree gave a disappointed mew. The thin branches whipped in a way that they should not have been able to do.

"Bronwen."

The voice was unknown to me but it tore at my heart and pierced a memory I had long lost. I stumbled over my words. What did I even call her? When she had died she had still been "mammy" and when I spoke of her now to other people she was "mam" or sometimes "mum", the more Anglicized version. Never did I say mother, with that stiff formality.

But I called her mother now.

She laughed. "Mother? I'm your mam, Bron, I always have been."

"Where are you? I can't see you."

"Come closer. I will show you."

My foot raised off the ground but a black wingtip brushed my cheek and I stopped. That was a warning.

"Bron, Bron, come closer, come say hello to your mam, Bron."

"Why are you in the willow?" I asked and suspicion grew in my mind. This was not following the pattern of my usual interaction with a human spirit. They didn't usually toy with me; that was more the inclination of other entities entirely.

"You know well why I am here; *she* trapped me here, but you can free me." The voice hissed over *she*.

"No, you were not trapped there … only a part of you, only the power that was in you. So what am I talking to? I want to talk to my mother. My whole mother. That was why I was led here. That was what I asked for."

"I am her. I am *here*. Come now, Bron. The promise was broken. We need to restore the balance."

There it is again. The Unbalancer, I thought. *Is this who they meant? This evil thing in the tree? And what promise does she … it … mean?*

"You're just a part of my mother," I said. "The dark part, the evil part."

"You cannot think that your mam is evil," she said, wheedling. "No good daughter would think that."

"Maybe I am not a good daughter," I said. "Or at least, not

the daughter that you want me to be."

"Bron!" The voice changed, lowered, and became broken and rasping. She – no, definitely it – was trying to sob but it didn't really have the emotional capacity for anything other than falsity and the cries were unconvincing. I was unmoved.

I stepped back a few more paces. This was not my mother. My heart ached. All that remained in this blackened willow was a small, dead fragment of the evil that had once resided in part of her. That was key: *part* of her.

This was not my mother.

Not all of her, at any rate.

It wasn't a sad thought. In fact, it had given me an idea. Perhaps there was a way to solve all of this without actually having to drop Evan and his cronies into a deep pit.

Maybe I could restore the balance.

Maybe it was this insight that had been the reason for me to come here.

I crouched, and leaped, and flew home.

***

I tumbled back to my place in the willow cave. The fire was still burning. My journey had been brief; in fact I think that only ten minutes had passed in the outer world. The time-space of the otherworld was strange. It might have been hours that felt like minutes, or the other way around.

I had wanted to meet my mother but I only met a part of her. Oddly, I didn't feel disappointed. I mused on that as I watched the flames burn down. That meant, to me, that most of her had passed on wherever she was meant to go. There was no lingering residue and why would there be, so many years later? She had followed the usual path, like most people did when they died. It was as it should be. If everyone hung around in the gaps between the worlds, roaming as restless spirits, the place would be impossibly crowded.

When the embers were safely out, I got up and stretched. I was not as disorientated as I usually was after an adventure like this, so instead of going back into the kitchen, I crept out onto the road. The lights were still on inside the house, and I suspected that someone – likely Dilys – was waiting up for me, with some food and a hot drink to earth me.

I had a flapjack in my pocket. I munched on that as I walked the night streets of Llanfair. It was full dark now, and there was an orange glow over the centre of town from the street lights but that faded as soon as I left it behind. My eyes adjusted to the pale glow of the moon though I stumbled once or twice. I headed south once more, out into the less familiar lands which were, recently, becoming more known to me.

I headed to the barrow. I wanted to see it again, but not through my other world eyes.

And as I suspected, my nocturnal activity had drawn someone else out to the Neolithic site.

He stood there on the roof of the mound, with his arms folded, making a large black shape against the paler black sky. He watched me come across the grassland, and I heard him sigh heavily as I got close. I stopped and craned my neck to stare up at him.

"Good evening, Gruffydd," I said. "Nice to see you again. Nice night for a stroll."

"I felt you poking around here earlier," he said. "I'm on alert because of what's been happening, of course. What were you up to this time?"

"I was led here when I asked Her if she could bring me to meet with my mother," I said.

I don't think he expected that reply. He sighed again, and came down to stand on my level. When he spoke, he sounded gentle. "Oh, Bron. And did you?"

"No. There is a small fragment of her left in that tree, but that's all. The fragment is … not nice."

"Don't let that trick you into thinking bad things of your mother," he said.

He was going to say more but I waved away his well-meaning platitudes. "I know, I know, don't worry," I said. "I'm not about to have some existential crisis over the whole thing. It isn't my mother in that tree. Ha, I did all my soul searching years ago."

"And did you find it?"

"My soul? Yeah, it was at the bottom of a teapot," I said. "It's all fine. Hey, though, as you are here –"

"Which you knew I would be," he pointed out.

"Well, yes. As you are here, I wanted to ask you, why did you come to me when you found the barrow had been breached and Maddie taken inside? Why didn't you go to the police?"

He laughed. "Just roleplay that conversation for me, then.

'Nine-nine-nine, what's your emergency?' 'Oh, yeah, an ancient monument has been opened and someone's being held inside by magic. There are demon traps and everything. Bring a couple of candles and maybe a book of spells.' That would work."

"Adam would have come out to help, without question; he was even on duty. And anyway, you're twisting it. You only needed to say 'abduction' and they would have been there, sirens blazing."

"You suspect me of more involvement, don't you?"

"Of course I do."

"Look, I panicked. Yes, me! I didn't know what was going on. I knew the barrow was opened, and I felt a presence within; I have animal messengers, the same as you, and they conveyed to me that it was Maddie, but that was all I knew."

"You didn't know that Evan was inside?"

"I wasn't sure until I got closer with you and then I felt his presence. He's pretty distinctive. I suspected it would have been him, of all of the possibilities, but I could have been wrong. I just thought that the most useful person in that situation would be you and not that daft rag Sergeant Polly Jones."

It was as good an explanation as I was going to get. I huffed anyway.

"Bron, listen. You hold yourself up to high standards, and that's fair enough, but you can't expect everyone else that you know to be as rational and logical as you think they ought to be. We're all only human."

"Even you?"

"Yes, even me."

Perhaps he had made a mistake and he really had reacted in the heat of the moment. Maybe I was seeing conspiracies where they were none.

"Okay," I said at last. "Next question. The Unbalancer."

"What of them?"

"Do you know who they are? Is it me? Was it my mother? Is it the evil part of her that resides in the tree?"

"It might have been your mother but I wouldn't like to assume so. It's in their Book of Dooms."

"They mentioned that – it definitely exists, then?"

"It does but it's likely to be the drug-fuelled scrawlings of decades of mad men. Most of these magical texts are."

"So you've not seen it," I pressed.

"No, and I'd rather not. As well as lunacy it's probably absorbed the evil intent of all its contributors over the years."

"We have to do something," I said. "And maybe that involves getting hold of this Book of Dooms and destroying it. Don't you realise that Maddie is probably still in danger?"

"Of course I do!" he said, angrily. "Why do you think I'm here now? I'm taking extra care to keep an eye on things."

"That's not enough. What are we doing, passively waiting for them to make another move? He took her once. I don't think he'll stop now. No. I'm going to act. I'm going to restore the balance. Surely that's the only way to destroy The Unbalancer."

"And what if *you're* The Unbalancer?"

"Well, obviously I won't literally destroy anyone. But like the fragment in the tree is not my mother, whoever is The Unbalancer, well, that's not their whole being, is it? All I have to do is balance things again."

"Those are just words. What exactly do you mean? Pratting around on some cosmic see-saw?"

I didn't know but I was sure that the answer would come to me. I squared up to him. "There's evil trapped in the tree, right? Evan and possibly the others want to get hold of Maddie again. My money's on Evan. Maybe just Evan working alone. Looking at the history, their predecessors wanted Ceri's magic so surely they now want Maddie's magic, right? Maybe they want to use it to release the evil from the tree. That would make sense."

"You're making that up as you go along."

I rubbed at my forehead. The events of the night were catching up with me and now I felt cold, and tired, and hungry. The flapjack had worn off, and I shivered. "Balance, balance; that's what it is about. I'll restore the balance. I'll come back to this tree in the daytime and … perform a ritual to counteract the evil that lingers in there."

I didn't expect a round of applause from Gruffydd but I had hoped for something different than his actual reaction: he gave a dismissive, barking laugh.

"You idiot. You of all people should know that it's not a simple playground game. You're talking as if you can plop a load of happy thoughts on one end and it will cancel out the bad stuff."

"I know it's not a see-saw. It's a circle, though, and…"

"Bull crap, Bron. It's not even a circle. Don't you know that by now?"

"Yes it is."

"It's a spiral, you fool. It's always a spiral."

That tugged at my mind. Yes, a spiral had movement and direction – an energy travelling up or down. "Well okay," I said. "But even a spiral can be out of balance and not spin correctly."

"It's a spiral in a web," he said. "Go home and sleep on this. Because it's a spiral in a web, and you're not alone as the spider in the middle."

I didn't get a chance to ask him what he meant. He knew that it would bug me, but he turned away and strode off. I half-heartedly ran after him for a few metres, but my head was spinning and my stomach almost sick with hunger now. I had to slow down and he was soon lost in the darkness.

He had done that deliberately, I thought. Now I was going to dream of webs and spiders and spirals.

If I managed to get home.

With a weary sigh, I plodded on.

TWELVE

I collapsed into bed after midnight. Everyone had gone to bed but there was half a cold meat pie waiting for me on a plate, a jar of pickle with no label and a vinegary smell, a glass of lemonade, and a teabag in a cup ready for hot water. I couldn't be bothered to brew up but I took the food and cold drink to bed with me, and when I woke early the next day, I was covered in pastry crumbs.

Someone had woken me up.

"What's up?" I muttered, struggling upright in the bed and dislodging the plate onto the floor, where Harkin pounced on it to inspect it for more food debris.

Dilys was standing at the bedroom door, and she looked strained. "I know it's early and you've had a late night, but you need to come downstairs."

I reached for my dressing gown but she stopped me. "No, get properly dressed. You will probably need to go outside. I won't have that man in this house."

"Who?"

"That Evan Morley."

That lit a fire under me. I dragged jeans and a baggy sweatshirt on, and ran down the stairs, dragging my fingers through my hair. "Where is he?" I demanded as I shot through the kitchen.

"Waiting by the front door."

I didn't use the front door. We never did. I ran around the side of the house and came out on the pavement. Evan was standing on the doorstep but my footsteps made him turn as I arrived.

"What do you want? Get away from our house."

"Hey, hey." He spread his hands wide like he was demonstrating that he didn't have a weapon. But I didn't trust a single inch of him. "Good morning to you too. Come on now, we're past that little incident with Maddie, aren't we? You all over-reacted."

"No, I will never be over it. How dare you say we over-reacted."

"Let's move on. You know about us. You know about your mam. She was one of us too. Come and speak with us, properly, and hear our side of the story. You are fair and honest, aren't you? We've got a lot to offer, you know. We've talked it over and we think this is the best thing to do. No one wants war, right? You're probably all about peace and stuff."

Me, peace and stuff? He didn't know me at all. "Are you … are you recruiting me?" I asked.

Evan cocked his head. "Um, yeah."

"Get the hell off my property."

He stepped away from the doorstep and across the

pavement, so that he stood in the gutter of the road, and grinned at me cockily. "There. Not on it. So, what do you say? Come and listen to us. Try and be reasonable."

"Don't you paint it like that, as if my refusal is some illogical act."

"But it is. You're a woman of power and you know that nothing is black and white. You've got us all wrong. Come and chat, relax, have a cuppa, and we'll tell you about Maddie. Anyway, she is in no danger from us. She never really was, and I can *promise* you we will never touch her again. I'll explain why I did what I did, and you'll understand that everything is going to be all right."

"Your promise means nothing. Get gone before I do something that *you* will regret." I added a stream of expletives. No doubt that Dilys was listening from a window and she'd tear a strip off me for this bad language but I didn't care. I unleashed a torrent that left him in no doubt at all.

"Fine, fine, it's a bad time," he said. "You've just got out of bed and you haven't had a cup of tea yet. That makes people grumpy. Come around later, yeah?" He had lost his smile somewhat. He shoved his hands into his pockets and stalked away.

This was not going to be the end. I didn't like the way he glanced back and raked his gaze over the house, like he was assessing something.

***

"Hey, what about we all go out on a family trip?" I said brightly as I went back into the kitchen. Everyone was up. I tried to leave my unsettling feelings about Evan behind. This was not the holiday that Ceri had bargained for, after all.

Ceri and Maddie looked at one another sideways. Maddie was the first to respond with a smile. "Sure! That would be great. You'd like that, wouldn't you, mom? Revisit some old haunts?"

"Dilys said that Evan was outside," Ceri said, not half as brightly as her daughter. "What did he want? I don't feel safe. I'm sorry, it's not you or this place, but you know, everything that's been happening…"

I put my hands on the back of a chair and leaned my weight forward. "I totally know what you mean," I said. "But Evan said that no one is in danger…"

"Well, I sure don't trust him," Ceri said. "Do you?"

"No, not really. Gruffydd also thought that Evan wasn't going to do anything else. And he's going to speak to John. And look, we'll get Adam to come over and talk to him. We need to tell Adam everything," I added, glancing at Maddie. "He feels left out."

Maddie nodded. "I know, I have to apologise to him for yesterday. It's just that I don't know what happened so I don't want to give him half the information."

"I have a better idea," Ceri said. She stood up decisively. "Let's all go down to the police and talk to them. Maddie, I am your mother. You were *kidnapped*. Don't you see how big this is? You can't just shrug it off like it was nothing."

"But mom, maybe it was nothing."

"You were held in a barrow! Underground! With a madman! Why am I the only person who thinks this is serious?"

"I think it is serious," I said, and Ceri nodded at me.

Dilys sighed. "It is serious. The police can't do anything but let's go to talk to them."

Maddie did not look happy.

"Fine."

***

We went on foot in one large group, like a posse, thinking that there was safety in numbers. We walked down the pavement but it wasn't wide enough for us all to go in a row, four people side by side, so we moved like a tactical unit in a small bunch and the people that we passed detected the seriousness rolling off us and got out of our way. There should have been a dramatic soundtrack playing as we stamped along. Even Dilys was slapping the tip of her cane into the pavement with viciousness.

I wanted to walk next to Maddie but she was next to Ceri, in front of me, and not talking about the police at all.

"Are things much different to when you were here as a kid?" Maddie asked her mother.

"It's all the same – I mean, like, the important things are the same – but the details are kinda different," Ceri said. "Everyone sounds strange to me. You know, in the States, people can still tell I'm not American, but here, everyone treats me like a tourist now. I don't sound Welsh at all."

"Where do you feel like you belong?"

"California, I guess. I've lived there the longest time now. But also, that's because you're there, and Michael."

"But I am here," Maddie said, and my heart flipped a little.

"Sure but you won't be here forever, right?"

Maddie didn't answer and I glowered as I followed Ceri. I had to force myself to stop being so childishly jealous. But it put me in a bad mood – not the thought of Maddie going, so much as the realisation that I was so possessive – and I was finding it hard not to scowl as we entered the small local police station. I had never thought I'd get so attached to people.

There was a civilian support worker manning the front desk. We were lucky to have retained this station at all. It now operated as a base for a wide rural area, and so it was busier than you'd expect. There were always unfamiliar faces coming in and out, a rota of police officers and community support workers who covered many remote countryside beats between the mountains and the sea. Crime was fairly rare, but residents still liked to see the panda cars chugging through their villages regularly.

I recognised the desk officer; she was a middle-aged woman called Karen who had once taught at the local secondary school, until she'd suddenly exploded in a very public frenzy and stormed out of her job when the school had been forced to become an "academy." Everyone knew her, and it was said that she had halved the crime rate simply by being a terrifying first port of call in the police station. She had taught most of the local would-be criminals in the area, and she still struck fear into them.

"I'll call him for you," she said, without any other preamble. She prided herself on knowing everyone's business before they even were sure of what they wanted themselves.

"Thanks."

Ceri browsed the noticeboards – "Report suspicious activity near bird nests!", "Watch out for modern slavery!" and the rather more prosaic "Have you checked your tyre pressure lately?" And soon, Adam appeared, clutching a pile of cardboard folders.

"You could have left them behind," I said.

"Then you wouldn't have known how busy I am."

"Fair point. Okay, this is sort of about yesterday. But more. Look, we're here on a police matter."

His eyebrows shot up. He became efficiency personified. Karen frowned and leaned forward against the Perspex that separated her from the potential hordes of angry public. "You didn't tell me that! I thought this was a social call."

"You didn't ask. You assumed," I said. "And why would all four of us come to see Adam?"

She looked aggrieved at having missed out on some information but there was nothing she could do about it. Adam led us to an interview room that only had enough chairs for him, Dilys and Ceri to sit down at. Maddie and I stood up. He offered to get more chairs but Maddie refused on my behalf, and muttered about some study that said sitting down was bad. Adam flipped open a notebook. "I really am snowed under," he told us. "But go on. What's the issue? Maddie?"

We all spoke at once, words tumbling over one another. He did his best, scrawling out our concerns and complaints in a long rush over the paper. When we were done, he tried to read the notes back to us.

"Okay, so you are saying that … yesterday, after the barbecue, Evan Morley kidnapped Maddie and took her to an underground, um, thing, this barrow, and would not let her go, until she was rescued by Gruffydd, and Bron, and Ceri. Why on earth didn't you tell me all this right away? I mean, why didn't you ring the police right then? This is a very serious allegation. Have I got that right?"

"Yes," said Ceri.

"Well, kinda," said Maddie, and she looked uncomfortable.

"How did he take you? By force? Look, everyone else be quiet. I only want to hear Maddie's side of the story."

Maddie shook her head. "I honestly can't say if it was by force or not. Remember when we were all at the garden party," she said.

"I was there," he pointed out.

"So they chucked that stuff on the fire and everything was confusing. I had a headache and I was tired."

"I remember," Adam said. "At first we thought you'd gone to bed."

"Yeah, no. I did go for a walk into town, and yeah I guess I was being a petty by walking off like that, and anyway, they both followed me – Owain and Evan – and they came up beside me in town and we got talking. It was mostly Evan talking. I really didn't want to talk with him but he kept on following."

"Did you tell them to go away?"

"No, of course not."

"Why not?"

Maddie looked at Adam in confusion. I stepped in. "Adam,

the papers are full of stories about women who tell men to go away and then they get murdered or something."

Adam tapped his pen on the paper. "That really hardly ever happens, and certainly not here, but okay, okay! I'll accept you didn't want to potentially cause an issue. Sorry. So how did you end up in the barrow?"

"I don't know," she said helplessly. She explained how Owain had gone to get her a drink from a shop, and she was left alone with Evan, and that was all she could tell us with any certainty.

"Did he drug you?"

"Maybe. I don't know," she repeated helplessly. "We walked, my head hurt, and then I was in the darkness and he was holding on to me and telling me stuff. Maybe I went along with it. Do you see why I didn't come to tell you straight away?"

"Once you were there, though, you couldn't get away?" Adam pressed on. "Obviously I can't put this in the police report, but between ourselves, was there magic involved?"

"Maybe but I don't know. I felt ill. It was dark and I didn't know where I was, or what was going on. What do you expect me to have done?"

"Right, right. And then Bron, you went and got her out…?"

"Gruffydd knew and he came to get me," I said carefully.

Adam put his pen down with a sigh. "Okay and no one even thought of calling the police there and then? You called a blacksmith instead of me? *Really?*"

We all looked at the floor in embarrassment.

Adam groaned. He picked his pen up again and flicked it

around in circles. "This is difficult but anyway, I will take it seriously, and I will get that Evan Morley in for questioning, and I'll get his side of things, and give him a warning, and I'll keep you informed, right?" There was a barb in that. He would keep up informed even though we hadn't done the same for him. He went on. "I am going to need to get signed and written statements off you all. Maddie, are you in ongoing danger, do you feel? Has there been anything else? Has he made any further moves or threats against you? And do you know why he did any of this?"

"I don't know."

"Yes, she is in danger," Ceri said forcefully. "Honestly, we should be on the next flight back to the States. I'm going to look into it today."

"No, please don't, now this investigation is open," Adam said.

I nearly whooped, and then felt bad, because America was the safest place for Maddie. I swallowed my elation back down. But all I had to do was destroy the Book of Dooms and somehow incapacitate Evan Morley and then Maddie could stay in Llanfair – easy!

Ceri mumbled a curse word and Maddie elbowed her in horror.

Adam said, "Is there anything else I need to know?"

"No."

He stood up. "Right. I'll go and speak to Evan, and I'll get back in touch about these statements," he said. "I really have to go now – I'm late for a meeting – but we'll get this all done as soon as possible. Maddie, phone the police station any time, if you feel remotely threatened. I will impress on Evan the importance of staying away from all of you. Okay?"

"A restraining order?" I asked.

"Nothing so formal yet but of course, that's an option for the courts in the future. It's not something I can do."

We had to be happy with that, and we filed out into the street.

***

We all went straight home. Ceri was talking about flights back to the States, in spite of Adam's warning, and Dilys had started wittering on about scarecrows. In an effort to distract Ceri, I proposed that we all spent the afternoon in the garden, making our creations for the upcoming festival. "You have to stay for that," I said to Ceri and Maddie.

They agreed, although Ceri had some degree of hesitation in her voice.

"Look," I said, "Evan won't come around to the house. If he does, I will go out and deal with him magically, and Harkin will scratch his eyes out, and you lot inside will phone the police, okay? We'll do everything right." Maybe letting your cat attack someone wasn't exactly 'right' but I would claim it was an accident because after all, no one can control cats.

It turned out to be a pretty pleasant afternoon, in the end. I managed to make a straw cat that stood about two and a half feet high, and it scared the living daylights out of Harkin at first. He went stiff-legged and jumped around it like he was on a pogo stick, with his tail held straight up like a bottle brush, challenging it to a moggy duel.

Maddie made a pair of slender and beautiful scarecrows, a couple, representing a farmer and his wife. Her glamour meant that she was naturally artistic. Dilys continued to work on her horrifying vision and her "improvements" just made her scarecrow increasingly X-rated. I began to plan how I might accidentally set fire to it. Someone had to think of the children, after all.

Ceri worked half-heartedly, and her scarecrow was nothing more than a few articles of clothing, partly-stuffed. Still, it was enough to occupy and distract her.

Dilys began to sing a version of "John Barleycorn", and as long as you didn't listen to the meanings behind the words, it was a pretty good rendition. Maddie said, "You know, I miss live music. I used to go to see bands play all the time, didn't I, mom?"

I didn't want that to become a reason for her to leave, and it jogged my memory. I'd seen the posters for some event locally. "There's something on tonight," I said.

"In Llanfair?"

"Yeah. There's an open mic night in a pub for folk musicians."

Ceri and Dilys both snorted with laughter, but Maddie was politely interested. "Is it gonna be traditional stuff, like harps and all that?"

"Probably," I said, as she seemed keen for the idea.

"Can we go?"

"You're not safe here," Ceri said.

"I am," Maddie replied. "Mom, listen. The whole Evan thing is getting way out of hand. It was a stupid thing, a trick, a joke, he's an idiot. If he had wanted to harm me, he would have. So let's stop obsessing about it, and just get on with our lives."

"You don't understand," Ceri said. "There's more to it."

"So tell me already."

Ceri pushed her hand through her hair and looked up at the sky. "Oh, you know what? Just go."

"Come with us, mom."

"I am tired. So yeah, maybe I am over thinking all of this. You guys go and have fun, all right?"

It was awkward. But Maddie nodded. "Right, okay. We will."

That should have been that.

It was a shame what happened later that night.

***

We had a late evening meal. The heat of the day, and the fact that we'd spent the afternoon in the sun, made us soporific and lazy. No one wanted to eat until the air had cooled down. We lazed around, and eventually I rustled up a meaty risotto. We sat down to eat at around seven o'clock, and Dilys brought out a dusty bottle of wine from somewhere. The label had faded but it was a rather nice and spicy type of Shiraz, and by the time that Maddie and I left for the pub, Ceri was relaxed with the alcohol, and Maddie herself was chipper and upbeat.

I hadn't taken Maddie to visit many pubs, at least not at night. We'd enjoyed a fair few meals in pleasant country pubs during the day and in the evening, as I had tried to show her what the essence of Britishness was – shaggy dogs, open fires, pickled eggs in a jar on the counter, that sort of thing. She'd enjoyed the dogs and the fires.

But a town centre public house, which didn't serve food beyond packets of crisps and pork scratchings, was a different sort of place. There was a crowd of people standing outside, smoking, and we held our breath as we plunged through the smelly air to get into the pub. We went into a small hallway that led off to the toilets at the back, and the main bar to the left.

It was already crowded. There was nowhere to sit, so I left Maddie propped by a window while I fought my way to the bar to get served. It took quite a while to get the barmaid's eye, and by the time I got back to Maddie, the first singer was taking his spot in the corner set up for the musicians. He had a hurdy-gurdy, and a determined expression.

And very little musical talent, as it turned out, but he made up for that with an awful lot of energy and thankfully the hurdy-gurdy is not generally an amplified instrument, no doubt under some rule of the Geneva convention, for the welfare of all humankind.

Then two women got up to sing. They looked like sisters, and one played the fiddle while the other sang a mournful song from the Irish tradition which was mostly about death, sex and loss. In fact, almost all the folk songs that I knew of – and that we heard that night – were about those topics.

"She's a great singer!" Maddie said. "She can carry on all night."

Alas, that was not to be. An old man who was mostly grey beard came up and half-chanted, half-sang a very long piece that was hilarious and moving in turns.

"Are you enjoying yourself?" I asked her.

"Yeah, it sure is different." There was a sparkle in her eyes and a genuine smile on her face, and I felt good to have been the cause of that. She drew strength from music, and this evening was clearly reviving her.

I had no warning that Owain had approached. I think, had it been Evan, all my senses would have alerted me, but Owain sidled into our space and took us both by surprise.

He looked awkward. He grinned, showing his teeth, but his eyes stayed wide, and his grin morphed into an apologetic grimace. "Hey, so, uh, how's the gate?"

"Fine, thanks. Tell me everything you know about Evan Morley," I said.

"Oh god, no, him? Look, I am really sorry about him."

Maddie said, "When you came out from the shop and found us gone, what did you think? In fact, was it a set-up? Are you in it together?"

"No! I only heard afterwards that he had taken you to the barrow. He shouldn't have done that. None of this is anything to do with you. He just acted on impulse without thinking." Owain shook his head and his voice was strong. "Please, please, believe me when I say that I didn't know, and I wouldn't have gone along with any of it. I just walked with you in town because … well, mostly because I didn't actually want to leave you alone with Evan."

"Because you knew!"

"No! Because he's a nobhead."

I nudged Maddie. "He's telling the truth, isn't he?"

She nodded. She could detect it better than me, but it didn't take a psychic to see the shame rolling off poor young Owain. "Anyway," he said, "so you're okay now?"

"You tell me," she retorted.

"Evan won't do anything again," Owain said with a fierce edge to his voice. "I will swing for him if he does, anyway."

"Very noble of you," I said drily. "Is this your local drinking den? Or are you following us?"

He looked startled at that accusation. "Folk night, isn't it?" He brandished a sheet of paper at us. "I've got a new song."

"Then it's not folk," I said stiffly. Maddie, I noticed, was looking less spiky.

"Of course it is," Owain said. Suddenly we were surrounded by a whole group of interested people wanting to get in on the conversation. The live music had stopped for an interval so everyone could stock up on drinks, and I noticed even Dean hovering on the edges. Of course – public music and song attracted druids like pie shops attracted me.

"Yeah," said a woman with very long straight grey hair. "We are the folk! We are the people! It's a living, vibrant tradition…"

Maddie hung on to her every word, and I went to the bar to buy us some more drinks.

The evening went by rather quickly. At one point, Dean and Maddie fell into conversation about different musical scales which completely baffled me, and I took the chance to grab

Owain and haul him into a corner between a jukebox and a cigarette machine.

He protested in vain.

"Shut up," I told him, holding his upper arm firmly enough that it would probably raise a bruise. He was too much of a gentleman to fight back properly against me. "I need to know about Evan."

"I told you, he's an idiot and he acted on impulse. Maddie was there, and he saw a chance to pretend to be all powerful, but he's not."

"Does he have magic?"

"Not really." He hesitated, and I squeezed harder until he began to speak again. "John Morgan Driscoll, he does."

"I know that."

"Me, no, only the poetry and song."

"Are you a druid?"

"No, no. I just have the everyday magic that anyone with a talent for something has," he said. "And John is birds, obviously. But Evan … he's studied and he's tried and he wants to be magical but anything that he can do, it's just out of rote and ritual but it's not really coming from inside him. Does that make sense?"

It did. "Why is he so … like he is?"

"Why are any of us, though?"

I sighed. "Okay, what about this group of yours?"

"You'll have to ask John about that."

"I tried," I said. "He blew me out. So now I am asking you."

"You can rip my arm off but I can't tell you anything," he said. "But we're not evil. We're neutral."

"You have to pick a side."

"Why?"

I couldn't answer that. "What about Benedict Rigby?" I asked.

"I never met him," Owain said. "But Evan did know him, years back. He's a bit older than me."

"Were they related?"

"Nah, I don't think so. Evan's got no blood relatives here."

"He grew up here," I said in surprise.

"Yeah, but he went from foster home to foster home," Owain said. "And it didn't suit him. I reckon they were all nice families, and that, but he never settled anywhere."

Something fell into place as I built up more of a picture of Evan. "The one constant was Benedict Rigby, then," I said. "This charismatic magician."

"Yeah."

"Do you know how or where he died?"

He looked surprised. "Er… no? Why would I?"

"No reason." I let go of Owain's arm. "Thank you for your time," I added lightly, and turned away, deep in thought.

"Hey guys, what's up?" Maddie came up to us. The final singer had finished, and the pub was now noisy with conversation and laughter. She was pulling on a light jacket and looked tired all of a sudden.

"Owain was just reassuring me that Evan was a random lunatic and no threat to you," I said, staring hard at Owain, who nodded frantically.

"So you said before. Come on, Bron, it's time to go."

We linked arms, mostly as a gesture of defiance against Owain, and left the pub. Outside the air was cool and welcoming. Maddie was a sensible drinker and had been alternating with soft drinks, and both of our heads were mostly clear.

"Do you still fancy him?" I asked her.

"Fancy," she repeated, giggling. "I am so going to say that all the time when I go home."

"Don't go home."

"Hey! Not yet. Ignore my mom. She has these wild moods, you know? She focusses on, like, one thing and goes on about it, and then – boom – it will be something else. She'll be staying for a while. And so will I."

"I'm glad to hear it. I'd miss you."

She squeezed my arm. "Are you okay? I mean, talking about emotions and all…"

"I am fine. So come on, about Owain …"

"Nah, not after what had happened. I know he says he didn't know anything, but he's a friend of Evan, so … no. He's cute enough and all, but no."

I left it at that. We hurried on, and when we got home, I was surprised to find that Ceri and Dilys were still up and in the kitchen. Another empty wine bottle decorated the table, and both women seemed floppy, hazy and happy.

"Have fun?" Ceri asked.

"Yeah. It was good."

"Let's have a nice cup of tea before bed," Dilys said, and made no move towards the kettle.

"No thanks – I won't sleep," Maddie said. But my blood

was mostly caffeine anyway, so I filled the kettle and set it on the range. Ceri got herself a glass of water. The atmosphere was relaxed and congenial, and the air was still and quiet.

It felt like a little moment of pure family bliss.

Harkin had been dozing in a cardboard box by the range when he suddenly leaped up and stood, quivering, and staring directly at me.

Danger outside was the overriding impression. The blissful feeling was shattered instantly.

He was indicating that it was danger aimed at us all, not something that was particular to him or cats in danger.

Alcohol didn't affect me like it affected most people – I enjoyed the taste, but I rarely got drunk. I did get hangovers, though, which seemed like a really unfair bargain. So I was the most sober of all of us, and certainly far more sober than Ceri and Dilys. Maddie was more tired than drunk, and she wouldn't have been able to detect the same danger that I did.

"What's up with the cat?" Ceri asked.

I decided it was not the time to tell everyone that there was some unnameable threat hovering outside. I got up and said, "Oh, I think Harkin wants me to help an animal in distress. You know what he's like. You all stay here. I'll go out and investigate."

Ceri and Maddie tried to protest, but Dilys waved them down. "She's right. Hang fire."

I went to the utility and picked up one of the walking sticks that lived in a bucket by the back door. Dilys followed me, and said, in a low tone, "No, not that one. Take the walnut wood."

"Oh god. Is this the one you keep mentioning that has a

knife in it?"

She laughed. "No, but it's proper hard wood, you see, you'll fetch them a wicked clout if you hit them with that one. Look at the knobbly bits. Brilliant for hitting people. Aim for bone that will break easily. I felt the same thing that you did; there's no injured animal out there."

"Shouldn't you be the sensible one and tell me to just phone the police?"

"Nah." She cackled at me, and went back into the kitchen, and I was not particularly comforted by her little pep talk. Still, I did take the walnut walking stick. It felt warm to my touch almost immediately.

I crept silently out of the house, and reached the gravel side area. This was an issue. I didn't think I could walk quietly over gravel, but I took my time, lowering each foot steadily and slowly. The sense of impending doom made my head throb. There was something out there, but curiously, I didn't feel like there was any immediate danger to me. If my life was at real risk right now, I would feel a sharpness in the air, a grey-metallic twang to the atmosphere. The overriding sensation I currently felt, though, was more of a general oppressive warning. I wasn't going to die right now – but I had to take care.

And whatever was creating this feeling was not alive.

There were no people or animals outside that I could detect.

That, in itself, was very strange. Surely I should be able to feel the warm outline of a bird hiding in a bush, or a mouse creeping along, or a fox probing the rubbish – insects, moths, spiders at least.

There was nothing at all but my own reflected essence. Or at least, there was nothing *alive* out there. I drew my energy in on myself and threw up a circle of protection around my body. I was on my own land, and aided by the house spirits, but I begged for a little more, and there appeared a golden sphere around me, not visible to the naked eye but it was there nonetheless.

Finally I had reached the end of the gravel and moved onto the pavement. I put my right hand out and touched the corner of the house, and it seemed to pulse back at me, a reassuring throb. There was only one orange streetlamp out here, as the road was now a rural one and wound up into the hills beyond. It cast a glow that only emphasised the edge of the darkness. It was usually easier to see at night if there weren't any street lights, because the on-off nature of their placement played havoc with your night vision.

This light was enough to see what was causing the odd feeling.

On the opposite side of the road, ranged in a line facing the house, were three tall black sticks shoved into the grassy verge. There were no houses opposite to us – just fields and then hills.

I did not cross the road to get any closer. I might be reckless but I don't actually have a death wish. I moved along the pavement, keeping my hand on the house, just my fingertips lightly resting on the stone.

The poles were about the height and thickness of broom handles. They didn't end with brushes at the top, however. Instead there were small curved shapes at the tips, and ragged strips of something that moved like fabric – ribbons, perhaps –

ruffing below the curved objects.

They had not been there when we came back from the pub twenty minutes ago.

All the bad feeling was coming from them, and I knew what they were. I was surprised to see them here in Wales. These were not of any Celtic tradition. We had some unpleasant ways of cursing people, generally involving the skewering of innocent frogs and floating them in particular wells, or so on. What I was looking at, though, was a northern Germanic or Norse artefact – these were *nithing* poles.

I paced my way back again, wondering what to do. Nithing poles, or curse poles, were set up to direct a curse upon someone, and these three were definitely aimed at our house. I knew that the strange curved ornaments on the top would be the heads of some poor creatures. In legend and saga, those animals would be horses. I suspected from the size of them that I was looking at the heads of squirrels or maybe large rats.

Who erected these evil things? My money was inevitably on Evan. And now what should I do? The curses would increase in strength over time, channelling their energy and pointing it at our house.

Though he could hardly expect them to last very long in the daylight. I didn't think the local council had an 'occult paraphernalia removal department' but I was pretty sure someone from the Highways section would be along to take them down. Passing motorists would soon be on the phone to the council, complaining about a "new type of stealth speed camera infringing their human rights" or some such paranoid nonsense.

From all that, I could safely assume that they were meant to scare us rather than actually cause real harm.

I hefted the walking stick, drew in a deep breath, tapped the house once more for luck, and launched myself across the road in a screaming frenzy.

I ran straight at the first pole and whacked it hard. It didn't break the pole but it fell over and the animal skull was dislodged from the top. I didn't hesitate. I kept running, my arm out holding the walking stick, and smacked the second pole with all my force. It, too, fell over. I let momentum carry me on to the third pole and brought it to the ground.

Then I turned around and jumped hard on the broom handle, but it did not snap until I kicked one end of it up onto a rock, and then slammed my feet in the middle. I repeated this with the other two poles.

I stepped back and got my breathing back under control. Already the cursed feeling was dissolving out of the air.

"Well done," said Dilys, coming up behind me on the pavement outside the house. "I told you that you wouldn't need knives."

"What are you doing?" Maddie said. Ceri was next to her, holding her daughter protectively around the shoulders.

"I thought this was all over!" Ceri rasped. "Something is going on." She peered into the gloom.

I hastily moved along the grass verge and scooped up the three animal skulls. I would cleanse these and bury them properly. The last thing we needed now was a bunch of vengeance-fuelled ghost squirrels.

"I'm just tidying up," I said. "Nothing happening. All done." The three warm skulls sat in my hand and I put that slightly behind my back. My other hand waved the walking stick, and that focussed everyone's attention. "There wasn't any animal out here. Hey, there's Harkin. He looks pretty relaxed now."

Everyone turned to witness Harkin who had paused on the path to perform some personal ablutions of a contorted nature.

So we all went back inside, and I knew Maddie and Ceri suspected me of something. Especially Ceri. She had just been relaxing, and now this.

I put the skulls in a cage in the utility room and braced myself, as I went into the kitchen, for more questions. I looked over at Dilys, hoping she'd help me out, but she had decided to cut up some fruit and make an impromptu punch – because where normal people open a new bottle of wine, or put the kettle on, she decides that a summer street party drink is what everyone needs. Of course. My half-brewed tea lay forgotten now.

Ceri took a big gulp of her wine, and drained her glass. She said, "Come on, Bron. Don't treat me as stupid. What the hell was happening out there?"

"Okay. There were curse poles," I said. "But I brought them down. It's okay, and I don't think they were going to work anyway. I think it was a warning. They wouldn't have lasted and they didn't have power." Well, they did, but I had dealt with it.

"A warning to us?"

I rested my chin on my hands. "Actually, I think it was to me. I think it was Evan, making a point…"

"Why would he target you? You weren't the one dragged

off into a barrow," Ceri said. "Oh my god, this place…"

"He wants to recruit me," I said.

Ceri and Maddie gasped but Dilys said, "Aah, of course," and we all stared at her until she shrugged. "How strong do you want this punch to be?"

"No one wants punch, Aunt."

"I am happy to drink it all myself. I'll manage. I'll make it very strong, then."

Ceri made a strangled sound. "Bron … it might be directed at you, but it might be actually aimed at me. There's more to all this than I've told you. I'm sorry."

Dilys nodded, like she knew all along.

I bit my tongue. I wanted to demand all the truth, right now, but people didn't work that way. Oh for that truth serum! I waited for Ceri to speak again.

"Mom?" Maddie prompted.

"I broke a promise," Ceri said. She looked down but I could see that she was flushed. It wasn't totally the wine's fault.

"She mentioned that," I said. "She said a promise had been made. So it was you?"

Ceri looked up, startled. "She mentioned that? Who are you talking about?"

"I rode the hedge, and I spoke with my mother. Part of her, at any rate. I don't think I met with the real spirit of her – that's moved on. So, what promise?"

Ceri had gone as white as the plates on the table. "What else did she say?"

"Rambling nonsense," I assured her. "I paid no heed to it.

Like I say, it wasn't the real person. But who did you promise? And what?"

"I promised the vicar."

"Horatio?" I asked.

"No, no, that was not his name. I wouldn't think he'd still be here. He was old, then, you know. He'll be retired or dead now. But I promised him that I'd … oh, I just want her to be safe," Ceri said.

She meant Maddie, but I also guessed that she meant my mother, too. She had promised to keep Lowri safe but she said she'd broken that promise.

She hadn't kept her safe. Her own sister.

"This new vicar, Horatio," Ceri went on. "He'll help us, won't he? I can't risk losing my daughter. I need to take her home as soon as I can. I see that now. But in the meantime, he will protect us from curse poles and evil in the night… because I can't."

"But we can," I said, indicating Maddie and Dilys. "You don't need to panic and flee, you really don't."

Ceri shook her head. "They will take whatever revenge that they can," she whispered.

I said that we'd speak with Horatio. The police couldn't help but maybe the vicar could.

THIRTEEN

"No. Absolutely not."

I was stunned.

I was sitting in Horatio's comfortable living room, surrounded by more cushions and fleece throws than an average homewares shop contains, and gaped at him.

The vicar was tall, round, solid and utterly obstinate. "Bronwen, my lamb. I will help you in any way I can."

"But you just said no."

"Because I cannot help you in matters of … your chosen path in life. Now, if this were a church matter, then yes; but when you speak of barrows and curses and shades trapped in willow trees, then no. What do I know of these things? I do not want to know, in truth. There are traps in there, for a man such as I am. I will not fall into them and I will not let you lead me there."

"But your predecessor helped Ceri."

"I do not live up to my predecessor's actions, nor that of any person. And I am not responsible for him. I cleave only to my Lord and Saviour. I will pray on this matter, my lamb, but I do not see how I can be of any practical help."

"I am not asking for practical help," I said, wondering what that might entail anyway. A really loud and intimidating hymn sung outside Evan's bedroom window? "But I do value your advice."

"You would not value this advice," he said. "And nor would it surprise you." He smiled suddenly, and his expression was mostly kind. "What do you think I would say to you?"

I felt like a sulky teenager as I kicked my heel on the carpet. "That I should let Maddie go back to America with her mam, and totally ignore Evan and the others, and also stay away from Gruffydd."

"Yes, almost all that – except for the blacksmith. He is trustworthy, you know."

"He's not … like you."

"Luckily, few people are. That is also a blessed relief to my bishop, who would not want to handle more of me. No, though I do believe that Gruffydd's priorities are his own matter, yet he will always look out for you and he will do nothing that directly harms you."

Directly? Somehow I really didn't find this as comforting as Horatio intended it to be. But I thanked him, and wandered out into the summer day, and pondered my next move.

I had to act before *they* did.

We were not victims and we were not ever going to be targets.

***

I went back to John Morgan Driscoll. I felt, between him and Evan, that he was the sanest of the two. I didn't even knock at his front door. I went straight around to the back, and surprised him, cradling a red kite in his hands.

"Bron! Hey, I was thinking of calling in on you," he said.

"I'm not joining your weird cult. I told Evan and I'm telling you. No."

"No, not that," he said, and thrust his present package forwards. "Please, will you take a look at him for me?"

So I clicked right over into professional mode, and though I thought for a second that it might all be an elaborate ploy to get me to let my guard down, I soon discovered that the kite was injured, and that he really did need my help.

He had a wing tag that was black, marking him as one of the Welsh populations. These birds are highly protected all over the UK and you can't even take photos of their nests without a licence. John worked hard in conjunction with the authorities and I could easily put aside my differences with him to lend my support.

The bird was listless. John passed him carefully to me and I bent myself around him, feeling his tiny rapid heartbeat. There was a foreign substance in him.

"Poisoned?" I said, half to myself.

John said, "No, he can't be. He's been mostly raised by me since he was brought here at six weeks old, and he will be released very soon – as soon as he's well."

"There's something in him that ought to not be in him."

"Magical?"

I shook my head. "No. It's of human origin … soft and grey."

"What?"

I squeezed my eyes shut. "Lead," I said at last. "He's being slowly poisoned with lead."

"He's only been with me for a month and a half. And there is no lead in the cages."

"What do you feed him?"

"Carcases that I get … Owain's been shooting, and so has Evan. Legally, mind you. They check on me, and I'm all above board. You ask your policeman fella."

"I don't doubt it. But what about the lead shot in them, the carcases?"

"You're joking, aren't you?"

"No. Take more care over their food," I said. "He's so young and it's built up badly. His liver is damaged but it will be repairable. You'll need to keep him here a little longer, and pay attention to what you feed him."

"I had another sicken and die recently," he said. "You might be right. I did read something in one of the journals but didn't take a deal of notice. Long words and short on sense, I thought. Anything more you can do for him?"

"I can give him some strength to keep going," I said, and John stayed quiet as I bent to my task.

It took more out of me than I had realised, and when I handed the kite back to John, I felt faint. He hurried and made it comfortable in a warm box in one of the cages, and when he got back to me, I was sitting on the concrete with my back against a timber upright. He crouched down so that he could speak to me on my level.

"Are you okay?" He was genuinely concerned, though mostly because he probably didn't want me to pass out on his property or something.

"Yeah, I just need a moment."

"Thank you for that."

"Of course. It's what I do. Anytime."

"Can I get you anything?"

"Um … I should eat something. Anything quick and easy like a bit of fruit."

"Banana?"

I nodded, and he darted off into his house. When he came back out, he had a banana, a chocolate bar, a can of fizzy pop and a thoughtful expression.

"When you're up for walking, will you come and see something with me?" he said.

I straightened up. I was just unwrapping the chocolate bar but I stopped. "Where? And why? Forgive me for not trusting you, but you've got form."

"I know. And I want to make it up to you, and explain a few things."

"I asked you to explain before. You didn't."

"I can show you. Come to the barrow with me."

"Not bloody likely. This was Evan's line of persuasion too. I am not joining you guys, end of story."

He sighed. "Please. Come and see what's written in our Book of Dooms."

"That's where you keep it, is it? In the barrow?"

"Yeah."

"Not, like, in a library or on a bookshelf like normal people?"

"Nope."

"Damn you."

He gave me a lop-sided grin, and I was struck by his sudden openness then. He hardly ever showed emotion like that. And he knew that I was going to agree to it.

If I had been able to use a mobile phone, I would have sent a text to Maddie.

But I couldn't. I couldn't do anything but ignore my gut feeling, and trust this untrustworthy man.

***

"Tell me about you and your group and this magic of yours," I demanded, once I felt strong and revived by the food. "And I want you to be honest." John walked slowly enough that I could keep up without getting out of breath. It was a pleasant summery afternoon, and we could have been a couple out on a stroll.

That was a horrible and unwelcome thought. I should have been enjoying the summer with Adam.

"We're deeply misunderstood," he said.

"Do you have a name?"

"Not really. We don't believe in labels. The thing is, as soon as you label something, you begin to define it. And a definition has a boundary. It includes and it excludes. So you naturally begin to restrict what that thing could become. A label limits any future potential for growth. Do you see?"

I did follow his train of logic, worryingly. I agreed with it, in the way that he presented it. So I felt sure I had missed some important flaw in his rationality. I tentatively agreed out loud. "Okay, fair enough. But do you have a core belief or central tenet?"

"We don't believe in absolutes or extremes. Everything is a mix of good and bad. In fact, these are human worlds we apply to things that don't deserve such value judgements."

"Maybe," I said, already feeling out of my depth in this pseudo-philosophy. "But if we don't strive for something that most people have agreed to see as 'good' then we have anarchy."

"So?"

"That's bad."

"Says you."

I shook my head in frustration. I felt sure he was wrong *somewhere* but I couldn't express why – I knew he'd tie me up in knots of words.

Luckily we were approaching the barrow, and the conversation shifted.

"Are you allowed to show me this?" I asked as we reached the open stone-bordered entrance to the dark heart of the place.

"We don't really have rules, as such, so yes. I can do as I please. Wait here."

I was glad of that – I had no intention of following him into the barrow. I remained at a safe distance so that he couldn't even spring a surprise attack on me and drag me inside.

I scanned the horizon around me. It was the sort of summer day where you really want to be finding a nice springy bit of meadow grass, and lying on your back, with a book by your side which you keep meaning to read – but don't – and maybe an ice-cream and a cool drink and some snacks. If there is any noise beyond distant birdsong and insects, it might be a low-playing radio – nothing loud or obtrusive.

And here I was, instead of all that, poised to flee for my life in case something demonic emerged from a Neolithic barrow.

"Here we are." John came blinking out into the light again, and he held a very large hardback book in his arms. It must have been larger even than A3 size, more like a book of maps than anything else, the sort of book that has its own special section in the local library. It was bound in a dark brown mottled skin, much like leather.

Oh. I wished that I hadn't thought of that word 'skin'. I had to ask.

"You want to know what it's made out of?" He laughed at me. "It's calf skin, you idiot. Nothing weird."

"It's still a *bit* weird," I said. "You know, sticky-back plastic is way more practical and you can get it in rolls off the market pretty cheap. But anyway. So what did you want to show me in this book, then?"

He laid it carefully on a flat rock near the barrow's entrance. We had to squat down, almost side by side. He opened it up at the first page. The paper was beige, and crinkled, and smeared with marks and grubby spots.

"Oh."

"You sound disappointed?" he said.

"Well – I had been expecting illuminations, and illustrations, and fancy calligraphy. A bit of gold leaf wouldn't go amiss."

"This isn't the Book of Kells," he said. "This is a working grimoire, passed down from generation to generation."

"I can see the date on the first page," I pointed out. "1973 isn't some great unbroken mystical heritage, you know."

"Maybe not yet, but it will be. That's why we protect it, and add to it. It will endure. Everything starts somewhere."

"And Benedict Rigby started this?"

John nodded. "He had his faults and made some mistakes, but I reckon this book was one of the good things he did."

"I thought you weren't into good and bad."

He ignored that. It was infuriating. Any argument that he thought he might lose, he just overlooked.

I peered at the scribbles, faded and angular, that scrawled over the pages. It was fascinating stuff. There was a fragment of a rhyme, a recipe for removing piles which I hastily tried to remember, and a drawing of a frog. On the next page – John turned them, and I felt sure I wouldn't be allowed to touch this sacred object – was an outline of a human being and there were layers drawn around them, in different colours, labelled as the various "etheric" auras. On he flicked. I recognised some things, like tables of correspondences, and snatches of verse that I had heard from my Wiccan friends. There was a mash-up of things from other religions too. "Is there anything original in here?" I found myself saying.

He ignored my rude question. "Here. This is the bit you

need to see. This happened twenty-five or thirty years ago, it's not dated very well, and it refers to the Coming of the Unbalancer."

He wasn't wrong about the bizarre dating system. It was the apparently "Time of the Swallows" and just before the "Mists that Rose". Someone, somewhere along the line, had changed from a normal dating system to something more evocative, arcane and bloody useless.

"*She rose up with the land and in a halo of yellow she unset what was set, and bound what was free,*" I read.

"Yup," said John. "The blonde-haired woman unbalanced things."

The sentences were unhelpfully written in a spiral that wound tighter to a central point. I had to shift my neck like an owl to follow the words. The letters got smaller and smaller. "*If she do return again in that form or another, then* – what is this word?"

John bent over and squinted at my pointing finger.

"Hang on," he said. "Let's spin the book around."

But before he could that, we heard heavy footsteps approaching quickly, crunching on the dry grass. It was Evan Morley, and as soon as he saw that we were looking at the Book of Dooms, he began to run towards us.

John snatched up the book and closed it, holding it against his chest as he stood up. I leapt to my feet too, and went on the attack before Evan could say a single word.

"You set up the poles outside my house, didn't you?" I cried. "You little turd."

He laughed in my face.

I was furious. I was at the end of my tether with his mocking attitude and the way he could simply ignore me. All the anger and frustration came to boiling point inside me, and I planted my feet squarely on the ground, and thought of nothing but *truth*. Purple-tinged white flowers flooded my mind as I called on the four quarters for help. I shouted at him again: "Did you set up those curse poles? Answer me! I command it!" I unleashed truth at him and expected it to come back to me, threefold, sevenfold, ninefold.

He blurted out, "Yes," and then looked so surprised it was almost comical. Like a dog that unexpectedly passes wind, he couldn't quite understand what had burst out of him. He pressed his lips together tightly and frowned.

"Yeah," I went on, "you're not laughing now, are you? Now tell me, why did you do it?"

He fought the urge to tell the truth. I shot everything I could at him, dragging up energy from the earth and the air, letting my boiling blood fire the power right at him. He staggered back, and clamped both his hands over his mouth like a coquettish seaside postcard. His eyes were bulging and I heard him mutter into his palms.

"Why did you do it?" I screamed at him.

He muffled and muttered and danced around, buffeted by the waves of magic I was sending at him. The bottom of my stomach felt raw, like it was being scraped with sandpaper, and I knew I was depleting myself dangerously. But I didn't care. I opened up the space between us and sent him everything I had.

I could see it. I had never seen my magic in the real world

before – yes, there were echoes and ripples and sparks, sometimes, but they were more easily seen by the closed eye than the open one. But I had never shot such force before, and it arced in a silver-gold rainbow from my chest and across the space to him. He threw up his hands to ward it off, and it slammed him backwards. He tumbled across the grass and landed on his back on the barrow, his heels kicking against the small stones which rattled through the dry grass.

The dry grass which was so very flammable.

The tiny points of hot light jumped from patch to patch, igniting like a chain of glowing lamps. Evan was oblivious to it, as he lay winded, but John and I saw instantly what the danger was. I began to stamp out the small fires and John, instinctively, slammed the Book of Dooms onto the nearest incipient conflagration.

And he was blown backwards, just like Evan, by the blast.

Magical fire meets magical book: that's never going to go well, is it?

The fire that was created was a pale and cool one, but it consumed the Book of Dooms in a flash and then – pop – it was gone, disappearing as if in a vacuum. I ran on, stamping out the last few real grass fires, and then turned to check on John.

He was stunned but appeared physically unharmed. He got to his knees, and saw what remained of the Book of Dooms – nothing but a circle burned into the grass, and outside of that circle, the outline of a rectangle, about the size that the book had been.

Evan staggered to his feet. "What have you done?" he

gasped.

I pointed my finger at him, still drunk on my power. "I've done exactly what I will do to you if you come near any member of my family, or me, or my house, again! I lay this charge upon you now: stay away!"

He turned around and ran. He fled from me, and when I looked at John, he too was white in the face and full of fear. He hesitated for the barest fraction of a moment before he legged it away after Evan.

I collapsed to my knees, suddenly so bone-tired that I could have curled up on my side and slept until next Wednesday. I breathed in and held it, drinking in energy from the air itself. My heart was hammering so fast that I was feeling dizzy and it took me a good few minutes to calm myself down.

I was on all fours, and I looked up at the yawning blackness of the barrow.

I felt, then, that there was one thing left to do.

I crawled forwards until I was only a few feet away from the unnatural darkness within. There was no real evil in there, but there was nothing good, either. It was neutral, like Gruffydd. I lowered myself to the ground, lying flat out, face down, on the earth, and I stretched out my hands to the edge of the shadows.

And then I began to twitch my hands, curling and uncurling my fingers, drawing in the thickness of the shadows to weave it together. I pulled out ropes of invisible matter and I wove them into a curtain or door. With the last ounce of my strength, I closed the barrow. I sealed it, as it should have been sealed before, as it had been designed to be sealed for thousands of years.

I rested my head on the ground and I think I must have slept, though not for long.

When I came to, the back of my neck was sore and hot from the sun, and I felt queasy. I sat up and looked around. It was late afternoon now, and I needed to get out of the sun, and get a drink, and eat, and sleep properly. I took my time in getting to my feet.

I climbed unsteadily onto the top of the barrow and looked around. There was no sign of any return by Evan and John. No doubt they'd be back, soon enough, and they would find their secret little hole closed up and inaccessible. Maybe they could open it again with magic, but I didn't think they'd risk it, not after what I had done to them. Maybe they would come after me, but that would be foolish. No, John would not, and Evan would be too scared to try.

I looked at the burned patch on the ground and felt a wave of regret and sorrow. I treasured books, all books. I wouldn't even turn down the corner of a page to mark my spot – instead I'd use a succession of receipts and takeaway menus and random slips of paper to use a bookmarks. I had now destroyed a grimoire – and yes, I'd mocked its lack of historical significance but John had been right – one day, that could have been an interesting collection of magical craft. If nothing else, it was a fascinating record of spells and charms and impressions.

My eyes had little dancing dots in them and I blinked to clear my vision. I had to get home. I scanned the area around me, and my heart thudded when I saw, far on a distant rise, the outline of a male figure.

For a moment I thought that it had horns, and I realised it was Gruffydd. When he saw me looking, he raised on hand at me, and turned, and walked away.

Now I was alone.

What was that? An acknowledgment, a warning, a dismissal?

Had I really won? What did winning mean, anyway?

I dug around in my baggy pockets and located a homemade flapjack, wrapped in clingfilm, dented and elderly and slightly sweaty, but I wolfed it down, and began to walk back towards the town.

Fourteen

I wandered into town. I had some loose change in my pocket and I bought a drink from the first shop that I passed; it was yet another half an hour of walking to get home, and I was dehydrated. I drained the bottle, standing outside, leaning against the newsagents' wall, and then went back inside to buy another one.

As I left the shop the second time, I caught a glimpse of Evan who was walking along a street parallel to the one that I was on. He flashed past, walking briskly, his head down.

I was going to ignore it – I supposed that I had done enough to him today – but I nearly dropped my bottle when a polecat, long and lithe like a furry snake, shot out in front of me and undulated down the side road to where I'd seen Evan. I looked up as a piercing cry rang out and I saw kites wheeling in the sky above.

This was no kind of coincidence. I knew a portent when I saw one. These were practically labelled "omen" in luminous marker pen.

Ceri had babbled about a polecat. A polecat had visited her

in her dreams, all those years ago, and told her what to do about my mother.

And the kites were John's own birds.

I drank the whole bottle, dropped the refuse in a bin, and followed Evan Morley. I didn't even listen to my better judgement. I knew just what it would say, and I didn't want to hear it.

***

The caffeine and sugar from the two drinks did their work quickly. I'd pay for this excess in the morning, but right now, I felt as if I still had a job to do. I tracked Evan along the side street. He was heading for the east side of town, where the lower-lying land was given over to a few fields of arable cultivation. Mostly, it was just grassland that was mown for silage to feed the animals over winter, but there were a handful of fields of wheat, barley and oats. We were more about livestock farming than arable here, but some land was good enough for crops and not wasted on sheep.

I kept Evan as far in the distance as I dared to, without losing sight of him. He walked angrily – there was a definite fury in the swing of his arms and the stamp of his heels on the ground. I had seriously unsettled him. He moved fast, too, and I had to scamper to keep up.

He was impulsive, and now he was angry. I wondered what he was going to do. At least he was not heading for our house.

He went along the road that followed the line of the river

in the valley's bottom, and then turned sharp right and I was momentarily confused until I reached the same spot myself, and saw that he had taken a footpath that ran between two fields. There were scattered bushes along the field edge, and I was able to use the broken hedgerow as a cover as I went along the rough path behind him.

We were in a field of oats and it stood about four feet high. Evan switched direction suddenly and moved out into the field itself. I kept back in the hedge. He was risking the wrath of the farmer – I didn't want to be caught out there, and accused of destroying crops. Evan stuck to the gaps made by the track of the tractor wheels, but he was clearly visible as he walked along in a straight line.

I couldn't follow him. If this had been maize, I would have been hidden by its height, but I didn't fancy crawling along on my knees to hide in shorter oats. I screened myself within a blackthorn, and peered through the spiky branches to watch Evan's progress.

He turned around and walked back, swinging his arms at the oats in frustration. He was talking to himself, and I ached with frustration that I couldn't get close enough to hear what he was saying.

Suddenly I realised that he was heading towards me. I ducked down and squirmed backwards, deeper into the hedgerow, the twigs and thorns scraping and scratching my bare arms and catching in my hair. I managed to get myself out of sight and he passed by quite close, seeming to be oblivious to my presence. I held my breath until he had gone and then wormed my way out of the hidey-hole. He was back on the road, and walking towards Llanfair.

I sighed, and felt foolish. I stood by the edge of the crops, and let my hands waft over the feathery, spiky tops of the oats. My mind was whirling in a chaotic mess – the sun and lack of food was making my thoughts collide slowly, like they were moving in thick sludge.

There was no point in following him. Finally my rational judgement had caught up with me and made its feelings known. Slowly I began to walk back to the road. As we were on this side of Llanfair, I realised that the quickest way home was to cut across the field. I looked around and there was no sign of a farmer with a shotgun. I decided that I would risk it, after all. I followed the tractor's path but still felt guilty that I was walking through the crops. I traced Evan's footsteps, and my fingers drifted through the oats either side of me. I didn't realise I was doing it, but by the time I got to the track at the other side of the field, I had gathered up a handful of long stalks in each hand.

I didn't drop them. I couldn't waste them. I decided that I'd take them home to make into a corn dolly.

I walked more and more slowly. In fact it's safe to say that I trudged. As I went, and got closer to home, I felt into gloomy thought.

Was Maddie safe now? I had done everything that I could – I had threatened Evan and shown him my power, I had destroyed their Book of Dooms, and I had closed off the barrow. Much of that had been rather more accidental than a true hero would have been, but even so, it still counted.

She was safe. I was sure that she was.

Ceri would not believe me. But then, Ceri was full of moods and passions. Soon she would go home to America. Maybe all this would be over for good, then.

My thoughts became circular and repetitive as tiredness claimed me. I was speaking aloud as I reached the back door of the house.

"Have I won now? Is it all over?" I said.

And the oats in my hand rustled, and whispered in a voice like the wind in the high trees: "No."

FIFTEEN

It is strange how you can hold everything together way beyond what you think that you are capable of – but the minute that you reach a place of safety, you fall apart.

That's what happened to me as I stepped into the kitchen.

I staggered, fell against the door frame, and my vision darkened.

At first I was surrounded by a cacophony of voices, and hands outstretched, demanding an endless stream of questions. *Where had I been? What had I been doing?*

Why did I look so terrible?

And then I was caught and lowered into a chair and food and drink was brought to me, and soft warm hands were placed on my shoulders until strength came back to me, and Harkin crept into my lap until security came back to me, and then I was led to my bed, and I fell asleep on the covers, and when I woke in the morning, the stalks of the oats were scattered over the bedroom floor like mediaeval rushes.

***

I lay there, on the bed, still in yesterday's clothes, and didn't move for a long while. I cast my awareness outside, and asked the house if there had been any disturbances. No. No curse poles, no attacks, no intrusions.

Harkin was with me, curled up alongside me, and when I reached out to touch him, he stretched and purred and gave my fingers the gentlest of licks.

I rolled over and looked at the oats.

Had they really spoken to me, or had I been so drained the previous night that I had imagined it?

And then I had to say to myself – yes, perhaps I had imagined it, and *that was no less real*. There was something true in the situation that I was missing. I closed my eyes and let my mind drift. There was a story, a folk tale, an old legend …

I had it.

I grinned to the ceiling, and sat up carefully. I had it! I knew the answer – well, an answer, if it wasn't *the* answer. Harkin looked at me curiously, so I petted him and told him what I had remembered.

"There was a king in this land," I said. "He was going bald, but he didn't want anyone to know. One person had to know, however, and that was his barber. Of course he swore his barber to secrecy and the barber was a good and honest man, and he did not tell a soul. But the carrying of this secret was a burden on the barber and so he went out walking one day and spoke his secret aloud as he went through a marsh, through the reeds and the rushes. No one there heard him, and he was relieved, and he carried on with his life."

Harkin watched me patiently.

"So," I went on. "Some time later a troupe of travelling musicians came to the king's court, and one of them had a pipe made of reeds. But instead of playing a merry tune, when the piper began to blow, the reeds instead spoke aloud – they spoke what they had heard when they were reeds in the marsh, and they spoke as the barber had spoken, and revealed the king's secret to all in the court."

Harkin waited.

I shrugged. "That's it, that's the important bit. As for the rest, I think no one was bothered and they all carried on as normal? Does that sound right?" It didn't sound entirely feasible. Most folk tales had far more betrayal, blood and death in them, like folk songs.

It was irrelevant. The story showed me that the oats could have spoken to me.

And, more importantly, they could be conjured to speak again.

***

The house was still and quiet. It was mid-morning, and I scavenged around the kitchen for food. There was a note saying Maddie and Ceri had gone out. I imagined that they were sorting flights to return home to America. I could hardly believe that Ceri had only been here for three days. So much had happened that it felt like a month. But I was not ready to lose Maddie yet.

The whereabouts of Dilys were a mystery but she was probably terrorising some poor innocent soul in the town, or plotting mischief with Elsie Delaney.

While I ate a sandwich, I toured around the utility room, checking on my real work. Dilys had fed and watered all the animals we currently had here, and there was one recent arrival of a sleepy tortoise in particular who now seemed ready to find a new home. Tortoises were quite a specialist area but I remembered there was a particular local man, a recluse, who kept these as companion animals so I didn't think there'd be an issue in rehoming this one. The two hedgehogs had gone now, and the bird was looking healthier. The cat had needed more specialist help and was now with the local veterinary surgery.

Otherwise, everything was peaceful. There was a note on a plastic tub in the utility room – "golden paste for Seren" – reminding me to make up some joint-easing stuff for an old sheepdog. But there was nothing else on the list.

This was good. I had a different task to do.

I finished my sandwich, and made a fresh cup of tea while I mixed up Seren's golden paste. The turmeric was an excellent remedy for all manner of aches and pains in dogs.

That done, and parcelled up ready to go, I returned to the kitchen, and swept a space on the table by simply using my arm like a bulldozer and shoving all the clutter over to one end. Then I spread the oat straws out.

They were green still, and not what you'd usually make a corn dolly from. That didn't matter because I wasn't after the aesthetic look of the thing. This was a practical and magical affair.

I separated the stalks into six piles. I'd made this as realistically human-shaped as I could, given the limitations of working with actual crops rather than something more sensible like clay.

I balled up one of the six piles and set it aside.

The other five sections became legs, arms and a body. I twisted and plaited, and wove them together. I used a few stray strands almost like a thread to make the joins more sure, and then frayed out the top part of the body so I could weave the balled-up head onto it.

Then I sat the strange simulacrum up, its legs straight out in front of it, resting its back against a tall pepper mill, and I looked at it.

It was already looking back at me, and I hadn't cast any magic over it yet. It was clearly ready to speak as soon as I could animate it.

My heart grew cold. All I knew of this kind of thing pointed to a place that I did not really want to go: blood magic. Blood was life, and to bring life to this thing, however fleetingly, would take a small sacrifice of my own. I picked up a knife that lay on the table and looked at it. It was a standard piece of household cutlery and was more likely to bruise than to cut, so I put it down, almost feeling some relief.

Was there any substitute for blood? Would spit do it? I was very reluctant to open a vein for the benefit of this thing. I cast my mind around the old tales, looking for an alternative solution.

Instead, I picked at a few strands of my hair, and pulled them out at the root, the sharp sting of pain almost edging into a flash of pleasure, fleetingly gone. I bit one of my nails, and pulled a small sliver free. I tied the nail into the head of the corn dolly using the strands of my hair, and then, with an effort, I spat onto its face.

I shuddered.

And, unnervingly, the doll shuddered back.

"Sorry," I said, half embarrassed that I'd spat on it, and half embarrassed that I was feeling the need to apologise to a bunch of oats.

It didn't have a face and I was suddenly rather glad that I hadn't tried to draw one on it. But the green-yellow stalks moved slightly where its mouth would have been, and I bent forward to hear what it had to say.

"I don't care what he says," the corn dolly whispered with the voice of the wind through the fields. "I've got to do something. She's the Unbalancer and she has to be made to pay for what she did to her sister."

I felt goosebumps. I said, "Who is the Unbalancer?" But I think that I already knew. I had always suspected who it was.

Anyway, the corn dolly couldn't tell me anything that it hadn't directly overheard. It was a recording device, nothing more. It repeated what it had said. "I don't care what he says. I've got to do something. She's the Unbalancer and she has to be made to pay for what she did to her sister. Someone has to act. John's a wuss. He probably fancies that Bron. She'll come running soon enough anyway. She'll see sense. But Ceri has to be stopped."

"What else did he say?"

The corn dolly repeated it all again, but the words came

more and more slowly like it was running out of steam, and it didn't add anything new to each repetition.

Then it slumped to one side, lifeless.

I picked it up very gingerly and carried it outside. I laid it in part of the hedge at the back of the garden, and thanked it, but there was nothing left there to acknowledge my thanks – its work was done and it was nothing but an inanimate object once more.

Then I stood in the shade of an old apple tree, and looked up at the hills that rose in grey-yellow parched ranks behind the house. Blooms of purple heather were making warm patches among the dry grass already. Summer would not last for ever.

And Maddie was not the target.

She probably never had been.

Evan was not lying. She had been a lure but she was not the objective.

I thought back to the night of the garden party. Maddie had been taken, but she had been out walking in the town. Evan must have done it on impulse, and seen it as a way of tempting Ceri to the barrow. That was why he and John could assure me that Maddie was not in any further danger – it was not her that he wanted, anyway.

No. Evan wanted Ceri. He always had done.

And he also wanted me, although for different reasons, and I felt a twitch of distaste at the remembrance of Evan's insistence that I was one of them. His insinuation that John fancied me was even worse. And I did not believe it, anyway. I thought of Adam, and realised I hadn't thought of him for a while, and I probably should have. He would have been to speak to Evan by now. I wondered how that had gone.

Still, I'd ask Maddie about John and if he harboured feelings for me, because she would be able to tell. Her glamour meant that she was attuned to matters of the heart. Unlike me, who was attuned more to animals, hills and pies. My stomach rumbled at that thought. It was time for dinner. Yesterday had been a strange day and I hadn't really looked after myself.

While I pottered around the quiet kitchen, I set my mind to the current problem. Ceri was the target – okay, I could see that. But really, the big question was *why*? She didn't have any power. So she wasn't any use to them. I could see why Evan might think I'd be a good addition to their stupid little cult, but Ceri had used up all her power a long time ago.

I felt such a strong pang of sympathy for her then. What must it be like, to know that you had magic once but you had given it all up? And you gave it up for some very troubling reasons, too. And now your daughter has power, but you do not? Your daughter is becoming who you could have been. Poor Ceri.

It really did make Maddie a more likely target. But they had said she was safe. And I hadn't detected a lie. Maddie was safe. I felt it in my gut.

And Evan had told the field of crops that Ceri was his aim.

It must be pure revenge, I thought. *She must pay – that was what he had said, more or less.*

Revenge really did have to be the most pointless waste of energy ever. I knew I had my faults, but the relentless pursuit of some imagined wrong from the past was not one of them. I really didn't know where people got the time or energy to fill themselves up with so much hate, and to devote so much of their day to getting even with someone. So it was hard for me to imagine the lengths that someone would go to, just to get "even" with someone else.

Then a new thought struck me. I dipped my slice of toast into a soft-boiled egg and considered the possibility that maybe Evan believed that Ceri still had some residual power, long-buried.

That would make more sense than just revenge, wouldn't it? I could imagine him acting because he wanted to use Ceri's power, somehow.

What if they got her, and found out the truth, that she had no power at all? Wouldn't they redirect to Maddie again, and go for her, instead? She had power, though she was controlling it much better lately, and would not be an easy one to use.

Either way, Ceri was still in danger.

I wolfed down the rest of my dinner very quickly. I had to find them both.

I accepted that it was time to get them both back on a plane and home to safety in North America.

***

I did a quick check of the house in case Maddie was in fact asleep in the front room, or Dilys was up in her bedroom learning to play poker or conjuring up the spirit of Houdini or making shell art or something, but there was no one around. I didn't lock the back door, of course – the house was protected enough. I rounded the corner of the house and nearly bumped into Adam on the pavement, who was heading my way.

I had been thinking of him. Maybe I'd conjured him up. It was good to see him, but I couldn't stick around.

"Hey, Bron, how are you?" he said with a grin.

"On a bit of a flier right now," I said. "Sorry – have you seen Ceri or Maddie around town or anything today?"

"No. I've not been on shift. I've got a whole day off. I spent this morning doing stuff for my mum and dad but I'm free now. I wondered if you wanted to come out this afternoon? I'll fill you in on Evan as well. I'm surprised you haven't been back to ask about that, actually."

"I was meaning to. Sorry, I would have loved to come out later," I said, already pushing past him. "But I really can't."

"Tomorrow? Tomorrow night after my shift? I'll get off early once the scarecrow festival is over."

"I'll let you know. You understand, don't you?"

He smiled briefly and coolly, and waved and I was gone.

***

I shot around Llanfair. My first port of call was the library because that's where they could get onto the free wifi and book some plane tickets, but they were not there, and the library staff couldn't remember if they had been in or not. I tried the café, and the market, and was just spinning around looking at the crowds outside the main shops when I saw a familiar dark head through the window in Sian Pederi's shop of hippy tat.

Maddie was hard at work, making up a new window display.

It was the usual mix of purple and black with skulls and fairies and rainbow things and glitter and gothic things and darkness. Sian sold whatever people were considering "pagan" at the time. Maddie had a great eye for art and design, and she was creating a rather effective waterfall from silver paper. There was also a growing scarecrow theme, ready for the upcoming festival.

I wandered into the shop, and she turned to say hi. She was kneeling on the carpeted ledge in the window.

"Hey, where's your mam?" I asked.

"She's taken the bus somewhere," she said.

"You're kidding me," I said. "After all that fuss about being in danger?"

"It's me, not her, that's the problem, though, right?" Maddie said. "We thought I'd be safe here, in public, you see. Sian agreed. Mom wanted to visit some old towns that she remembers. She'll be okay. They're not after her."

I felt a little dizzy. Ceri was the target. "Maddie, I've got something to tell you."

"What's up? Is she okay? Have you felt something? Surely I'd feel something. She's okay, isn't she?"

Her rising voice brought Sian out from behind the counter. "Bron, what's wrong?"

"Everything is fine," I said. How did I say to Maddie that her mother was possibly in danger from a lunatic who talked to oats, when we didn't know exactly where she was? It would cause unnecessary panic. "Does Ceri have her phone with her?"

"She does but she messed up with the roaming networks," Maddie said. "I don't think it works here in Wales. Maybe she fixed it now though. You want me to call her?"

"Please."

I retreated to the doorway and looked out onto the street while Maddie went to the back room and tried to call her mother. She emerged a few moments later. "Yeah, sorry, no luck," she said. "So you want to tell me what all this is about? You've got me worried, Bron."

I glanced at Sian. "Is Maddie due a break?"

There weren't many times when I felt well-disposed to Sian, but this moment was one of them. Without hesitation, she said, "Of course, right now, as it happens. Go on. We're not busy."

I towed Maddie out and across the square to the café, where we fought for a table inside and settled down with some cold drinks.

She looked at me with a mix of fear and curiosity. "What's going on, Bron?"

Sixteen

"I think I've sorted everything," I told her.

She cocked her head but didn't dare to risk a smile just yet.

"I've sealed up the barrow," I went on. "That's where they were getting their power from, Evan and John."

"And Owain?"

"Him, and whoever else was hanging on at the edges. I don't think he was a big part of it all. Owain is not magical. John is more about the birds. It's only Evan who really needed stopping, and I've done that. Yeah. Also, um, I kinda sorta accidentally destroyed their Book of Dooms."

"You did what?"

"I didn't mean to, but there was a little fire, and anyway, so, it's gone."

"Oh my gosh, Bron, they are going to be so angry about that when they find out…"

"No, no, it's fine. They know what I did."

"How can it be fine?" she blurted out. "You've seen what they're like. These are not rational people, Bron, and they are going to be *pissed*. You know? They won't let you get away with this."

"But they will, because … they've seen what I can do. You know, the fire and everything. I let them know that I could … stop them."

"What, did you threaten them or something?"

"Pretty much, yeah, I have."

She licked her lips nervously and sat back. She played with the half-full glass on the table. "Is my mom in danger, Bron? Tell me the truth now. I can tell if you are lying, remember."

I knew that. But I tried to deflect things. I couldn't say that Ceri was in danger when we didn't know where she was. I really didn't want to stress Maddie out even more. What would be the point of that? It would be cruel. I said, instead, "What promise was your mam talking about?"

"What, when?"

"She said she'd broken a promise. Do you know anything about that?"

"I don't. What do you think she meant?"

And I couldn't answer that either. I was thinking, *your mam made a promise to keep my mam safe. And she broke that promise. She broke a promise and I think that's the one she broke. I know it was to do with my mam. Instead of keeping her safe, she tore out the heart of power from her and bound it into a tree. Maybe that's what she had to do.*

Maybe it happened as accidentally as my burning of the Book of Dooms. What tales would Evan and John tell of me in the years to come? If Ceri was the Unbalancer, what would I become in their new Book of Dooms?

Who would come after me in the future, in ten years or

twenty, having read some arcane scrawl about me and my actions?

I didn't know the truth but I reckoned I knew *a* truth, a version of it, and in that version, Ceri and my mother were both bad – or at least, had made bad decisions – and were also both victims.

And Maddie was looking at me for answers that I was not yet prepared to give.

I would usually have included her. She could have helped.

But no; this would cause her too much pain.

I knew, however, that this was not something I could tackle on my own.

I craned my head and made a big show of looking at the clock on the wall behind the counter. "Oh, is that the time! I'm late. I'm supposed to be meeting Adam round at his place."

"What?" She narrowed her eyes and probed for the lie.

I was quick. "Yeah, he's got today off. He called earlier and asked if I was free to meet up this afternoon." That was true, and Maddie could only detect that it was true. She flared her nostrils.

"Right. You suddenly remembered?"

I jumped to my feet. "Yeah, with so much happening, hasn't it been hectic! Brain like a sieve, ha ha. I am *so* sorry. Look, don't worry about a thing. Your mam will be home soon. Um … yeah. I'll catch you later." And I threw down a few pound coins to pay for my drink, and I ran.

***

While Ceri was out of town, she was safe. I repeated that

to myself to reassure myself that everything was going to be all right. Evan was here, and she was somewhere else. That was a good thing.

Also, it was only Evan who was after her. He had mentioned John and I didn't feel that John agreed with what Evan was doing. I couldn't believe that of John.

I went in the direction of Adam's house but once I was out of sight of the café, I switched routes. Adam would not be the best choice right now. I didn't have anything concrete to tell him, and it was unfair to ask him to intervene in something that had no evidence.

I know he had been reading up on magic and everything, but I also wasn't comfortable with him knowing that I'd conjured a corn dolly – well, oat dolly – to speak, either. Now he'd learned a little more, he might jump to conclusions. I wanted to be a normal sort of girlfriend for him. And normal girlfriends didn't turn up demanded that someone was arrested because he'd spoken aloud in a field of oats.

I was in danger of isolating myself. I knew that was a bad idea. No one would think better of me for trying to take all this on alone. It was foolishness. And I'd made that mistake before.

So, this time, I went to seek help. Horatio had refused. But he had reminded me of one person that had power, and in spite of my doubts that still lingered, Horatio was probably right.

I headed out of town and along the track that led to Gruffydd's forge.

I felt very proud of myself for showing such good sense.

Seventeen

I used to come up here a lot. The forge was in a solid low building with a decent amount of hardstanding for parking outside. Gruffydd mostly specialised in ornamental ironwork, but he also shoed horses. Some of those horses were supernatural beings, however, and events over the past year had shown Gruffydd to me in a new light.

Sometimes, people reacted to me strangely once they knew I had magic. I used to think they were being silly.

Now I knew how they felt. I didn't fully understand Gruffydd's realm and it unsettled me. My visits to his forge had dropped off, and I regretted it now. I missed sitting in the low chairs, listening to his tales and jokes, drinking tea from disgusting tannin-caked mugs, and gossiping about the local population.

The big double doors were shut.

I paused. It was another warm day, so if he was working, he was bound to have them standing open. Even so, I went up to them and tried to open them. They were locked, as I knew they would be. I knocked, fruitlessly. I sent out my awareness to detect if anyone was around, and my heart temporarily leaped when I felt the approach of a man.

But it was not Gruffydd.

It was Adam, and he looked very angry.

He drove up the track, his car bumping around, and pulled up on the concrete. His window was wound down, but he didn't get out of the car. He cut the engine and leaned his elbow out of the window.

"I don't actually live here," he said, in a flat and unfamiliar tone. "This is Gruffydd's place."

My first thought was that he'd been influenced by Evan. The Adam that I knew was always friendly, happy and upbeat.

"I know," I said. "Um…"

"But Maddie just came around to my place, because she thought something was up, and she expected to see you there. Because apparently we had arranged to meet up this afternoon. And you told her that you were coming to see me. Instead, here you are."

"Oh – yeah, sorry, it was just something I said to her, because…"

He drummed his fingers on the hot metal of the car door, letting his hand dangle.

"I've hardly seen you for weeks."

"You came to the barbecue."

"That's been the only time for a while, and it didn't go very well. I could think of more relaxing times."

I was annoyed. "Hey, listen, Maddie's mam is here, and you work long hours yourself, remember."

"I know. Okay, the thing that has really got to me, though, is you brushing me off saying you're busy, but then ending up in a café with Maddie – yes, she told me – and then worst of all, using me as an excuse to abandon her there quite suddenly. You lied to her, about me, and came here instead. That's not fair on her, or me. So what's going on?"

Not this again. Way back, Adam had had a bit of a jealous thing going on about my friendship with Gruffydd. I think Adam was literally the only person in Llanfair who hadn't realised Gruffydd was gay. Although, thinking about it, that shouldn't even be a handy "excuse" to "allow" me to have male friends. That made me even more annoyed.

"Nothing is going on. I came up here to see an old friend, but he's not here."

"Why did you lie to Maddie?"

"I don't know."

He shook his head. "This is not like you. Ever since Ceri came over, you've been odd."

"Well, Maddie did get kidnapped, if you remember."

"Yeah, about that. Maddie herself doesn't say she was kidnapped. I spoke with Evan Morley. I thought you might come around to see me to follow up on that, as it happens. He denies there was any coercion on his part."

"So that's it? He's lying, you know."

"No, that's not it. It's on file."

"Wow. Big wow."

"Bron, you know how it is! She hasn't made an allegation. It was all coming from you, and Ceri and Dilys."

I sighed heavily. "Okay, look, I am sorry. Adam, I really don't want to argue with you. I was looking for Ceri. Have you seen her?"

"You came up here looking for Ceri? Is this another lie?"

"Well, no, I came to ask Gruffydd if he had seen her." And I came to ask for advice, but Adam wouldn't want to hear that.

Adam shook his head. "I don't know what to make of you right now. Let me know when you've got some spare time to talk with me."

"We could go out for a meal –" I began to say, but he cut me off.

"No, not at the moment. You need to think about whether this relationship is important to you. About how you take me for granted. And I really, really don't appreciate being used as some kind of cover-up." He fired up the car engine and spun it around.

I watched him drive away. My throat hurt.

I could make it all better again, and I would. I would tell him everything. I'd tell him every scrap of truth that I had.

But not today. I had to prioritise.

So now what?

I walked.

I walked down the track and back through town and out the other side. I hunted for omens and portents, seeking signs in the call of birds and the drifting of clouds. I hunted for polecats and kites, cats and snakes.

But nature's world of signs and symbols seemed dumb to me today, and in my quest for a message, I found myself heading over the heathland to the south of the town, but not towards the barrow.

I went towards the silver birch, Ceri's tree.

And I knew I had been following a sign that I had been unconsciously aware of, because as I topped a small rise and the view spread out before me, I saw that someone was already at the tree.

It was Ceri herself.

Eighteen

Ceri was dressed in a long white tunic and blue leggings. She looked fresh and modern, like a glossy magazine advert for Californian holidays. I felt sweaty and lumpen as I approached. I wondered if her magic, back in the past, had been glamour, like Maddie's affinity was. It would make sense.

She had her hands on the trunk of the tree and she was staring up into the branches above her, but she knew I was coming. She spoke as I approached. "This is my tree, you know."

"I know. Ceri's tree. I thought it was for Ceridwen but Billy put me right. Did you plant it?"

"Yes. Look how tall she's grown!"

"Why did you plant it?"

"It was part of my atonement for what I'd done." She dropped her gaze to meet my eyes.

"You are the Unbalancer, aren't you," I said, and it was not a question.

She nodded. "Yes. Did you not know? I would have told you. It's a hard title to bear."

"You are Evan Morley's target. Not Maddie."

Again she nodded. "I realise that now. I didn't, you know, at first. But it's why I haven't panicked as much about getting Maddie away from here. She's safe. It's only me they want. That's why I am not with her now. She's better without me."

"What else are you not telling me? Because I don't understand why all this is happening."

She shrugged. "I've told you everything, Bron. Believe me. You know the worst and I am so sorry. What else can I say?"

I took a deep breath. My mouth was dry. "When are you going … home?"

"After the scarecrow festival. The day after tomorrow. I'm sorry. I shouldn't have come."

That was so soon. I tried to keep my face impassive. Before I could say anything else, she spoke again.

"And Maddie doesn't know."

"What are you going to do? Drug her and kidnap her?"

Ceri blinked in surprise. "Er, no? I'll say goodbye in the usual way, but I just don't want her to get all upset beforehand, you know?"

"Hang on a minute. Is she not going with you?"

"She has a life here. She told me right from the start that she wanted to stay a bit longer. She's taking classes at the community college, isn't she?"

"Yeah, but… oh."

"She's not the one in danger, is she?" Ceri said. "Like I said, it's me. I'm the issue, I'm the problem, I'm the real target. Like you have worked out, I am the Unbalancer. What's done is done. And once I'm gone, things will get back to normal."

Except they wouldn't because now I'd done some unbalancing of my own. I'd burned books, sealed barrows, made enemies who meddled with dodgy magic, all that kind of thing. Still, there was no point in telling Ceri any of this. And anyway, I was doing a few little mental cartwheels of celebration – Maddie was going to stay here in Llanfair, at least for a while.

"Don't tell her," Ceri said. "She'll be upset. She thought I'd stay for a good few weeks."

"I won't say a thing. Are you absolutely sure that there isn't anything else you're not telling me, though?"

She shook her head and looked away.

It felt as if she were telling the truth but I just didn't know any more.

She looked like she was going to stay there by the tree, and I suddenly had a feeling that I was intruding. I stepped away. "Okay, well, I'll … see you back at the house for tea tonight?"

"Yeah, sure. And, thanks."

I wasn't sure what she was thanking me for. I waved it aside, and started to walk away. Then I stopped and turned.

"Ceri, you might be in more immediate danger than you think."

"How so? I know that I'm a target. That's why I'm leaving."

"But you're standing out here in the open. You should come back to the house with me."

"No, I'm safe here, by this tree. And I am sure that I'm safe while I am in open spaces, and public places, and daytime."

"No, listen, Evan Morley is out to get you. He … said so."

"He's full of big words but I really don't think he'll try again yet. It went wrong with Maddie. I know, now, that he was using her to get to me. And he made an impulsive act. He doesn't seem like a planner. He seems like a kinda sad case, you know? I might not have magic, but I can call on protection from the land, even so, you know, Bron; I'm not completely a victim. I'll be gone soon."

"Evan is unpredictable. Adam went to talk to him, but all they've done is 'put it on file.' I don't think that means anything."

Ceri was still shaking her head and smiling slightly. "Honestly, Bron, he won't come for me while I'm here at my tree. And he won't try anything tomorrow because it's the scarecrow festival – it's too busy. And then I'll be on an airplane headed home."

"You're not talking sense," I said with a feeling of impotent infuriation. "What about when you walk home, from the tree, though town? You're exposed then. What about tonight? You said he wouldn't try in the daytime, but… No. You must come with me, back to the house, and stay there, and not go out on your own." I felt like a mother telling her daughter off.

"I will *not* live my life in fear," she said. "Everything is a risk. Everything is calculated. We weigh up the odds all the time. I will come back to the house by public, busy roads. Okay, I agree to one thing. I will stay inside tonight – with you, and Maddie, and Dilys. That makes sense, all right? If Evan is going to try anything, he will be biding his time. That's another reason why you must keep my leaving a secret. By the time he's organised himself, come up with some plan, I will be gone from here. Okay?"

"You just said he wasn't a planner. He is impulsive and that makes him dangerous. What if he tries to attack Maddie again, to get you to come back?"

"He won't. Their issue is not with me – it's with me being *here*. Don't you see? I'm a threat while I'm in the area. They have to get rid of me. They don't need to destroy me. They only need to make me go."

"How are you a threat?" I pressed. "You have no power." And if Evan was only working on revenge, I thought, he won't be happy with her leaving. He wanted to hurt her.

"I am a reminder," she said. "You'll see. Once I'm gone, everything will be fine. It was all okay until I came here, remember?"

I chewed at my lip. I felt as if I was still missing something important, but I could not, for the life of me, work out what direction I should be going in. Everything she said was plausible. It was true. Two days, and she would be away, and that would be that.

"Will you come back with me now?"

"No," she said. She smiled. "Trust me."

I didn't trust anyone. But what could I do? As convinced of her danger as she had been, now she seemed blithely unconcerned. Moods and passions indeed. Why weren't people more logical and predictable?

I gave up. I turned and headed for home.

I decided I'd take the golden paste up to Seren the retired sheepdog, make a few other calls around the area, and then work on the scarecrows for tomorrow's festival.

What else could I do, after all?

***

The posters for the festival were all over town. One of the main roads was going to be closed, and there would be a parade of floats, all cumulating in the market square. There would be music, food stalls, and various competitions. Local businesses had sponsored prizes for the various age categories, and the whole town had got behind the festival. We did it every year, and it was a highlight of our summer. It was great for tourists, but we didn't do it for them – this was a celebration for ourselves, and it always had been.

I suppose the roots went way back to antiquity. The first of August was Lammas, or the old Anglo-Saxon *hlaf-mas*, which marked the end of the midsummer hay harvest. But it wasn't the big harvest festival, in spite of what some folks from the towns seemed to think. I couldn't blame them. If they got their pagan wheel of the year from books then it was often written down as a harvest festival. Those of us lucky enough to live in a rural area knew that it was only the start of the harvests. Different crops are reaped at different times. Lammas, or Lughnasadh to the revivalists – Sian's shop was full of cards with Lughnasadh on them, and I liked that – was a time when a loaf of bread was baked from the first of the crops. The harvest though would go on for weeks, ending in September.

I did like this time of year. It was a time of fruition, and while for anyone involved in agriculture it was one of the hardest times of the year, for most of us it was a time of relaxation and fun. Things were easier for me in one sense, as people and animals did not get as ill as they did in winter, because of the good weather. On the other hand, that meant I had less income. But it doesn't cost anything to lie on a sunny hillside and watch the clouds scud overhead, and so I didn't mind it too much. And there was always a few daft summer injuries, mainly alcohol-induced, to attend to.

I felt that Ceri was being foolish but on the other hand, I had to agree with her. Evan was an idiot but he wasn't going to do anything in broad daylight and within the sight of other people. I could not feel any threat looming. I could believe that his actions at the garden party – the gunpowder on the fire – was just a stupid trick, and his kidnapping of Maddie was an impulse that he had not thought through, just because he'd seen her in town, and she had been ill and vulnerable. He had annoyed his friends, Owain and John, and started to estrange them with his antics. John in particular seemed to have some kind of influence over Evan, and he would be a calming voice, urging restraint. He had promised to speak to him, as Gruffydd had. And Adam had. There were enough people urging Evan to stop.

And anyway, what would Evan gain from moving against Ceri?

He wanted to "stop" her and "make her pay" just out of silly childish spite.

He wasn't an immediate threat and soon Ceri would be gone.

And we could all relax then.

By the time that I got home, I myself was feeling almost relaxed and relatively chipper about things. I'd talked myself into a state of acceptance. I'd done what I could do, and warned Ceri, and followed Evan, and made my feelings very plain to John and the others.

There was very little to be gained from dwelling on any of it. I kept my senses alert but I could detect no threat at all. The house was long and quiet and welcoming. The garden was peaceful and secure. Harkin lay in a patch of sunlight, stretched out on his side on the broken patio slabs, and only half-reared his head to watch me enter the kitchen.

Dilys was sitting at the kitchen table. She had a pair of scissors in one hand, and a large pile of chopped-up fabric scattered around her.

"What are you doing?" I asked as I headed, by default, towards the kettle.

"Making a wig for my scarecrow. Is yours finished?"

"I've done some extra corn dollies and a sort of scarecrow cat," I said. "That one I started the other day. I'm going to put the finishing touches on it later."

"What has happened between you and Adam?"

"Nothing. Why, what have you heard?" I kept my back to my aunt so that she could not read my face.

"When the bathroom mirror misted up this morning, I couldn't see properly, and you know what happens then."

"Ah. What did you see?"

"A multiplicity of futures, and you in the middle, holding on to the strings, and you didn't have a clue which one to pull."

"So which one did I pull?"

"I don't know. You haven't done it yet."

Ugh. Fortune-telling was so frustrating. Why couldn't the Fates be a little more clear?

Oh, I knew why. Free will and all that nonsense. Whatever. I turned around to face Dilys and her wrinkled-apple face was impassive.

"Can you feel any danger coming our way?" I asked.

She shook her head. "I've been looking more carefully than usual. There is nothing threatening us today."

"Tomorrow?"

"That's the festival."

"I know," I said. "Will we be safe to go?"

"What can be done in plain sight of all the public of Llanfair?" she asked.

What indeed.

"I think me and Adam are having a bit of a break," I admitted at last.

"Who decided that?"

"Um. Him."

"What did you do to make him decide that?"

"That is not fair," I said. "We're both really busy."

Dilys started hacking at a long strip of paisley-patterned flannel. "Yes, well, you're busy with your head in your bottom, aren't you?"

"That is so rude."

"You did something powerful the other night. I felt it. I would have thought even the most non-magical lump of jelly felt it. Are you going to tell me what it was?"

"I have stopped Evan and the others accessing the barrow to draw on its power."

"And is Gruffydd okay with that?"

"Well, he knows about it," I said, remembering the figure on the hill and his raised hand.

"You might have swapped one enemy for another," Dilys remarked. She began to gather up the strips of cloth. "Perhaps you should have stuck with Evan and those lot."

"I don't want anything to do with them."

Dilys got to her feet slowly, one hand on the table while the other clutched the fabric. "Sometimes," she said, "the way to change something is from within. Like those wasps do to those animals, you know." With that arcane pronouncement, she hobbled outside to make her own scarecrow look even worse than it currently did.

I wasn't sure about the wasp thing but she was probably alluding to some horrible parasitical relationship. I shuddered. Not having immediate and ready access to look things up on the internet was something of a blessing, if I'm honest.

I took my fresh cup of tea and walked to the window. I stood by the sink and looked out through the towering hollyhocks and over the pink-white sea of cosmos flowers, and contemplated what else my aunt had said. I knew what she meant, in an instant. If I had "joined" with Evan and the others, she was implying that I could have changed their group. I imagined taking over, and setting them all right.

I would be a great dictator, I thought. *People just don't know what's good for them.*

Then I laughed. Tempting though it was, I knew it was not for me. I sipped at the hot tea. Maddie would be home soon, and Ceri would turn up. I'd cook a nice evening meal and we'd swap stories and get ready for the festival tomorrow. It would be our last day together, although Maddie didn't know that yet.

But I could keep the secret, for her sake.

She didn't know what was good for her.

It would be all right.

Nineteen

The evening passed without event or trauma. Ceri came home soon after me, and looked at me smugly. She had been right. She had been safe.

Maddie came in with cakes from Caffi Cwtch, and we enjoyed a pleasant evening though it was a more subdued one than the previous night, and there was no alcohol unless you counted Dilys's various "medicinal" drinks, which she didn't, and I wouldn't dare to question.

We had an early night. We woke to a normal day – no curse poles, or talking corn dollies, or anything.

We all went down to the town centre together on the morning of the scarecrow festival. It was a sunny, cloudless day, and already warm though it was early. Our scarecrows, and my scare-cat, were piled in a wheelbarrow which Maddie was pushing. Ceri walked alongside her, and Dilys flanked Ceri, tapping her stick on the ground with each step.

I brought up the rear. I was on alert, of course, but not overtly so. However I felt a chill when I caught sight of Evan Morley.

He seemed as if he had been looking for me. I saw him first, prowling around the crowd, scanning the little knots of people. When he saw me, he stopped. And then he grinned, and winked, and turned away.

He was up to something.

But surely not here, not today.

I had to put it from my mind.

He was just trying to rile me up, like a schoolboy wanting to get a reaction from a classmate. I would not let his infantile bullying affect me.

We took our scarecrows to the area set aside for ones that people had brought in. We had left one scarecrow outside our house – one of Maddie's gorgeous creations and too good to shove in a field. Many houses and most of the businesses had at least one scarecrow set up outside, and a lot of people had gone to the effort of making complicated themed tableaux. There would be prizes awarded for those when the judges made a tour of the town later that day.

But for now, everything was centred on the market square. Various pens were marked out and we found the one for scarecrows made by adults.

"Oh my gosh," said Maddie in awe as we passed the ones made by children. "The kids are, like, way better than us. I mean, look at that one!"

It was true. The age ten to fifteen category had the absolute best with a mixture of worryingly contemporary political figures and some amazing fantasy creations too.

"Hey, there's Adam," Maddie said suddenly and grabbed

my arm. She waved to him.

He was on duty, helping to organise the traffic due to the road closure. He glanced up and waved back at us, but didn't come over.

"He's busy," I said.

"We should go say hi!"

"He's busy," I repeated, and she picked up on my tone instantly, as I knew she would. She pulled me to one side. Dilys and Ceri were arguing, in a light-hearted way, about the best placement of Dilys's horror creation. I thought the best place for it was the bottom of a river, but apparently such a sentiment was considered churlish.

"Hey, so what's going on between you two?"

"Nothing," I said.

"Do you mean nothing as in, you're not dating any more?"

"That's right. I think. I am not sure. We're taking a break. That's the mature thing to do, isn't it?"

She narrowed her eyes at me. Her gentle probing glamour stroked me. I tried to shrug it off, throwing up some spiky defences, but she could slide in between them. "Well, you need to talk to him, because you've got something good going on together and you shouldn't be so quick to throw it away."

"Why do you assume it's my fault?"

"Er – because I know you."

I wanted to be mad at her, but it wasn't going to wash. "Yeah, I have been wrapped up in things," I admitted. "But I will change. I am going to do better. Just as soon as … the festival is over." *And your mother has gone*, I added in my head, but very quietly, just in case she had suddenly learned to be telepathic or something.

She smiled slowly. "Okay then. I'll believe you."

"Thank you. I know you've got my back."

She threw up her hands in mock horror. "Whoa, steady girl! Bron, being kinda nice? That's like, twice in two days."

"Shut up." I pushed at her and she pushed me back. We tussled like a pair of schoolboys but it was just a way of showing affection.

We were stopped by Ceri and Dilys descending on us. "It's time for the first round of judging," Ceri said. "Come on. They're doing the community groups first. Did you see what the senior citizens made? It's amazing."

We joined the crowd gathering around a stage that had been set up at one end of the market square. It was a large space and we all got a good view. The mayor and various local officials, including uber-business-woman Rachel Harris, made speeches brimming with buzzwords which left us all feeling a mixture of local pride and eye-rolling cringing at the clichés.

In a pen below the stage were the various creations of the community groups. There was a diverse mix of scarecrows. Don't be thinking they were all variations on Worzel Gummidge or something out of The Wizard of Oz. In fact there were some very artistic efforts. There was a life-size Shirley Bassey and two different Tom Jones (they were probably from the seniors), a footballer that I could not identify, a handful of very wide rugby players, the inevitably unflattering effigy of our local Member of Parliament, and an alien.

To be fair, that might not have been intended to be an alien, but the tentacles and things made me think it had ended up as one, however it might have started out.

There was also, in the middle, a very large scarecrow dressed as a traditional farmer.

Maddie nudged me. “Don’t look, but down to the right of the stage, there’s Evan and he’s staring at you.”

“How can I not look now?”

“Okay, kinda look like you’re not looking.”

I squinted and tried to focus my peripheral vision that way. Maddie was right. There he was, and he was certainly looking our way.

Maybe he was staring at Maddie. Or Ceri.

But a cold finger stroked down my spine. I felt, now, as if he *was* looking at me.

He had promised not to interfere any more.

I couldn’t help it. I looked directly at him. I was issuing a challenge as much as anything, of course. I wanted to remind him that he had said he wouldn’t do anything.

Since when did his word mean a thing?

He held my gaze. My vision seemed to narrow and focus only on him, as if I were looking through a telescope at him, and everything was dark at the edges.

He raised his hands. There was a yellow corn dolly there and he seemed to be showing it to me. It was in the crude shape of a person.

When he wriggled one of the stubs that represented an arm, my own arm twitched.

"What the hell?" I blurted out.

"What's up?" Maddie hissed. People turned around to glare at me, and tut, before pointedly turning around again to the announcements being made on the stage.

He must have seen the horror on my face, even from that distance, and he understood what it meant. He grinned in triumph as he lifted the other arm of the corn dolly.

My left arm flexed, a shiver running through the muscles. My mouth went dry. "That's the corn dolly that I made myself a few days ago, here in the town centre," I said.

"You made that? How has he got a hold of it?"

"I don't know. I … it was in my pocket. I must have dropped it." I searched back through my memory. "I might have dropped it in the barrow that time. Oh god." Because my remembrance threw up another fact: I had cut myself, and left my blood on that corn dolly.

"Maddie," I said, urgently, but in a low voice, "he is going to try and control me through that thing."

"He – what? He can't. No, put up a circle of protection. Let me help. Take my hand. Come on, stop looking at him. Let's get away."

But as I tried to step to one side, out of his eye line, he wrapped his fingers around the corn dolly's feet and held them tightly in his fist.

I remained rooted to the spot. I could feel the band around my own ankles. I would have screamed but there was a group of small children nearby, gazing at the scarecrows in the pen below the stage. This was not the place to cause mass panic.

"Maddie, I can't move," I hissed.

"Protect yourself! Where's mom and Dilys? I'll go find them. Stay there."

"I'm not going anywhere," I said desperately. While his hand held my feet, I could at least move my arms and head. I physically reached out, pointing my palms at the four quarters. I usually cast a circle in my head but I felt the need to move, as if in some kind of fruitless defiance against Evan's magical control of me. I called North for steadfast and solid and darkness and cold, and South for the power of fire and warmth and burning blood; I called East for the pure mental energy of air and West for the purification and rush of moving water. There was sky above and earth below; I was in my land, and on my land, and within my land – I encircled myself and called out, too, on another plane, drawing Harkin to me and begging for help. I must have looked like a right sight. At least most people's attention was focussed on the stage.

My feet tingled. I felt a trickle of power come up from the earth and it gathered pace, suddenly flooding my body. I began to ball it up so that I could use it. I planned to unleash it in a rush and break the bond between me and the corn dolly.

But before I could do that, the power that coursed through me was dragged right on out of me and crackled in the air as it shot over to where Evan was standing. The people around us felt something warm and spiky, and a few raised their hands to pat their hair or smooth down their clothes, or glanced around to see who had bumped into them.

Evan sucked the power of the earth and my own circle,

sucked it right across the market square and into himself, laughing and cackling with sheer triumph.

I gasped, my knees buckling. Maddie came to my side and Dilys moved around to stand on the other side of me, and they both grabbed me, trying to support me. "Stop him," I whispered. "He's using my own force. Break it, break the connection. Can you see it?"

But this was not my aunt Dilys's power and she could not do that. Ceri was standing in front of me, fear on her face, but she too was helpless.

Maddie could wash me with the gentle reassurance of glamouring, but what would the Fair Folk do here, for me? Not a lot. I remembered Ceri's dismissal of Faerie magic: could they stop a bullet? No.

And now Evan was walking towards us, drunk on the waves of energy that were crashing out of me and into him, holding the corn dolly aloft, and laughing loudly.

The prize-giving ceremony up on the stage was coming to an end. The DJ took over, playing some music, while the judges had a break. They would reassemble in a few minutes' time to look at the next category of scarecrows. People broke apart, milled around, headed for the drinks and food and toilets, and into the crowd came street entertainers – jugglers, mimes, people with puppets and magicians with flying packs of cards.

No one took any notice of me, on my knees, with Maddie and Dilys to each side of me.

Evan advanced upon me.

Ceri whirled around, so her back was to me, and she put up

her hands like a police officer. "You stop right there!" she commanded.

He was ten feet away from us. He smirked. He did stop, and he inhaled, puffing out his chest. Then he turned to look at the pen of scarecrows off to one side.

I could *see* the magic – my magic, damn it – whirling inside of him and he flung his arms up, shooting it out towards the stuffed straw figures.

They stirred.

TWENTY

"No, no, no." The babbling was coming from my own mouth. I fought for clear thinking. What could I do? He dragged the power out of me.

It was not my power. Everything was a loan, I reminded myself. A borrowing, a channelling; I was not the source of the power, I was just a vessel for it. "Lift me up!" I blurted out to Maddie and Dilys. "Ceri, Ceri, help us – get me off the ground."

The scarecrows were standing up now, and moving around, stiffly and jerkily. The people standing near the pen cooed with delight at this unexpected trick. "Robots!" they said and "Isn't that clever! What computers can do nowadays, well, isn't that lovely, eh?"

The scarecrows got more proficient in their sudden animation. They gathered at the gate of the enclosure, and I saw a small boy, eyes wide, say to his mother, "They want to come out!"

"Open the gate then," the mother replied, keen to be a full participant in this lively street entertainment. This is the age of wonders, after all. Flash mob, hidden cameras, YouTube; Maddie had explained so much to me. Everyone *knew* that the scarecrows were being controlled by some remote means but no one wanted to see the wires or the controls. Everyone was so very eager to be deceived.

The straw figures shuffled around, politely taking turns to leave the pen. Maddie hauled at me, her arms around my waist, dragging me up to my feet which remained rooted painfully to the ground. "Mom," Maddie called, "turn around. We need you."

But the scarecrows came for us. They made a circle around us.

No. They were making a circle, and closing in, on Ceri. She was a few paces ahead of us and the straw men and women were able to sidle in between, and encircle Ceri.

"Gah!" With an explosion of force, aided by Maddie and Dilys doing her best, I tore myself free of the ground and the connection was broken but the power was still being dragged from me to Evan. My circle of protection seemed to be useless.

And now he was draining me. He was taking the remnants of my power, and it was not being replenished from the earth. My head spun and I felt myself about to lose consciousness.

Maddie grabbed my hand. Her essence was light and laughter and song. Her grip was firm and I came back to myself, enough that I could stand and think more clearly.

"You leave her alone!" I screamed at the scarecrows.

"You don't know a thing, do you, Bron?" Evan said. "We have tried to show you but you can't see it."

"I do see it. I know everything. Ceri is the Unbalancer – yes, I accept that."

Maddie's hand squeezed mine in a sudden jerk. "Bron, she's what?"

"But it isn't a circle, is it?" I went on, and now I was holding on to Maddie as much as she was holding on to me. "It's not a case of tit for tat. She did this, my mother did that, now you do this, and I do that. Actually we don't have to carry on like that, you know? We can make this a spiral, not a circle." I knew what Gruffydd had been trying to tell me.

"Your mother was one of us," Evan said.

"My mother did an evil thing." I said it out loud. The world did not end. My palms were slippery. But I said it.

Evan said, "Well, that's subjective. After all –"

But I did not give him the chance to finish.

"She did an evil thing, and you can't dress that up in any other way," I insisted. "Maddie, it's okay. She did a bad thing but it's okay. We all do things that are questionable. I don't think she was a bad person. And after all, even your own mother…"

This bit was harder. I didn't need to say anything. I stopped. I just had to save Ceri, regardless of what she had done.

But I hesitated.

Ceri turned around. Her face was pale, with blotchy patches of red on her cheeks, pure terror flaming her skin. "And me?" she said. "Help me, Bron. I'm powerless. You know that."

I looked at her and I wanted to help her. But something had been bubbling away in me for a long time now, and I came out with it at last.

"I will help you. But I just want you to know that … I'm doing it because it's the right thing to do, not necessarily because it's for you. You broke that promise, after all. You promised to keep my mam safe yet you bound her power into that willow and stripped her of it all. I know you didn't have a choice, and I agree with you, but you broke that promise…"

She stared at me with wide-open pink-rimmed eyes. "Bron, I don't know what you're talking about."

"You said you'd made a promise …"

"Yeah. Sure. But not to your mom. I promised the vicar that I'd stop her. That I'd *destroy* her."

"What kind of vicar would want that?" I cried out, appalled.

"An old one of the fire and brimstone brigade. Thou shalt not suffer a witch to live, after all. That's what they say."

Maddie was squeezing my hand so tightly and I squeezed it back, just as firmly. "You promised to destroy her – I mean, come on, what do you mean by destroy?" I asked, nervously.

"Exactly that. Destroy. Utterly. But I broke that promise, Bron. I did not destroy her. How could I? He said it was the only way to save me and her own soul but I could not. I took her power but I let her … live."

"You did the right thing?"

"No, as you say, I broke a promise. You were saying that was wrong. Why is that suddenly right?"

Words tangled us up.

I could not fix this all by myself. I never could.

Evan, watching, rolled his eyes. "Are you done? I mean, this is all very lovely and that, but hey Maddie, you didn't seem to know any of this, did you? What a pair of cows they are, eh. Leaving you in the dark about it all. How do you feel about that?

They knew and they didn't tell you."

I felt her falter. Her grip loosened. As it did so, the scarecrows moved again, crowding in by slow degrees around Ceri.

"Come around here and get a better view, Maddie," Evan called. "Owain's looking forward to you joining us, Maddie. Bron, you come too. You always knew it was inevitable you'd join us. You know it, in your heart."

There was one other person with us.

We had forgotten her.

Dilys.

Old, ancient in fact – with the invisibility of an old woman, and the fury of long years, and the sheer randomness that was her very essence, she grabbed her walking stick and held it vertically, in the centre of her body, the head of it close to her chest and the tip pointing down at the ground. She walked around the scarecrows that were now inches from Ceri, making a solid wall of straw around her. She stamped her way right up to Evan and before he could react, she belted him firmly on the side of the head with her stick.

The crack resounded.

It staggered him and broke his connection to me, freeing me to jump forward. I plunged into the scarecrow ring, and elbowed them aside, grabbing hold of Ceri.

"I can't do this alone," I told her, "and you can't do this alone. Maddie, get here…"

Maddie said, from outside the circle, "What's going on?"

"Maddie!" we both screamed, Ceri and I, yelling as one

voice, and Maddie came to us, and we made a triad. Not quite the old maiden-mother-crone stuff but real life often fails to follow neat mythological patterns. We'd do the best we could with what we had. We were three, after all – and four, with Dilys outside, smacking seven shades of living hell out of Evan, and everyone around not quite sure what to do about that. There was something that stopped people wanting to lay hands on an elderly woman.

All the scarecrows but one had stopped moving now. Evan's channelling of my power had faded, but the biggest scarecrow seemed to be drawing on something different. I looked at it. This was the one dressed as a stereotypical farmer, with blue dungarees and a yellow checked shirt, and a tweed cap on its flat-eyed head. The fabric face rippled and I think it was screaming or laughing; it was hard to tell, and I didn't want to look too closely.

The other straw figures were falling to the floor.

This one seemed to inflate its chest and grow taller.

"Who are you?" I yelled, still clinging to Ceri and Maddie.

The red gash of its painted mouth twisted. "I am John Barleycorn."

The hairs went up on the back of my neck.

I knew what to do and I knew what was right – for this situation, this moment.

I said, firmly, "Then John Barleycorn must die."

TWENTY-ONE

Someone, at last, had dragged my semi-psychotic great aunt away from the gibbering Evan. I do not condone violence in any way, of course, but there was something very satisfying about seeing an elderly lady beat a horrible and irritating young man with a walking stick. That probably makes me a bad person, but I really don't care.

Frankly I see that particular vision of Dilys as one of my future life ambitions.

Evan pushed away the people who were trying to help him. He had a trickle of blood running down the side of his bruised face. He pointed at the three of us. "You will pay!"

"Yeah, so you've said," I retorted. "I really don't think so." I aimed a kick at the legs of John Barleycorn, who danced back out of the way.

That made me pause.

He was becoming, moment by moment, very lifelike. I didn't know where he was drawing his power from – possibly it was just something inherent in the time of year. After all, John Barleycorn *had* to die, annually, out in the fields, the god-king sacrificed year after year so that the new crops would grow again.

So I had to get him out to the fields.

I looked up and saw birds high in the sky, and they were circling.

They were waiting.

And a voice said in my head, very distantly, like an echo down a tunnel, "Yes."

I called the kites down. I let go of Ceri and Maddie, though Ceri whimpered and tried to grab my hand again. I raised up my arms and I called the red kites to me and they came, because they knew their purpose and this is what they had intended to do. It was a spiral after all. There would be balance.

If you've ever wondered how many red kites it would take to lift a scarecrow, it's more than you'd think, especially when the animated straw man is fighting back. There was a flurry of brown wings and razor-sharp yellow beaks. Feathers flew in the air, and there was a high piping call echoing around. The wings beat on the straw man and he croaked out a raspy protest, like straw being fed into a threshing machine.

I couldn't see him any more. The red kites covered him like a living blanket and the figure slowly began to rise in the air. As he was lifted up, I could see his booted feet kicked ineffectually.

The crowd around us was spellbound, cooing and taking photos on their phones. The electronic devices nearest to me fuzzed and made beeping sounds as they reset. I was hardly concerned with that. Instead, I turned back to Ceri and Maddie.

"He'll be taken out to a field. A field of crops. We need to follow him."

"How do you know?" said Maddie, and there was a world of hurt in her voice – not just about this, but about everything. What did I know, she meant, and how? Why did *she* not know?

And Ceri said, "What about Dilys?"

Dilys was on her feet, and clutching her stick. She was surrounded now by friends. Jemima was to one side, and Billy was on the other, with Alston from the café. Everyone knew Dilys. If she was hitting someone, people would think, then that person probably deserved it. She met my eyes and nodded. "I'm all right. You go on, now. Oh – you will need something."

"What?"

Dilys was turning around, scanning the crowd, with one hand on Jemima's arm to steady herself. "There, that stall, the historical society. Billy, would you?"

"What do you need?" he asked.

"Fetch me the sickle, love."

"Aunt, no!" I said in horror. "You were bad enough with your walking stick."

She grinned. Billy ran off and returned swiftly with a small hand-sickle, a curved blade on a wooden handle. He handed it to my aunt, and she passed it to me.

"It's not for me," she said. "It's for you. A sickle, a good honourable woman's weapon. Now, Alston, does your café serve brandy?"

"Of course not."

"But … *could* it?"

"Absolutely not." He sighed. "Oh, come on over with me then. I'll see what I've got in the back."

"Ooh, brandy," Jemima said. "Don't mind if I do." And she followed them.

We didn't have time to lose. The kites would drop John Barleycorn in the fields way before we could get there, but I wasn't sure what he would do when he was dropped. Would he stay, or would he try to come back here? The only place he could be taken were the fields of oats where I had seen Evan, and that's the way I went now, with Ceri and Maddie following.

I held the sickle in my right hand. It fitted. And I knew what Dilys meant for me to do with it, now.

Behind us, came Evan Morley too, and he was muttering and swearing.

At first a few people from the crowd came following behind Evan, thinking that it was some extension of the rather realistic street theatre that they believed they'd been watching. Most people, however, were attracted back to the stage where the mayor was rapidly getting on with announcing the next set of competition judging. The general public might have thought they'd been watching some amazing robotics but the organisers knew very well that something strange had been going on, and they wanted to cover it up without revealing there had been anything amiss. If people enjoyed what had happened, no doubt the organisers would be swift enough to take the credit.

I suppose the people in charge were assuming that there had been some hijack of proceedings. I'd find out later.

By the time we got to the road leading out of town and down to the valley, only Evan was following us. There was a dark dot in the sky far ahead, which I took to be John Barleycorn.

There was little traffic on the road, and everything was quiet, with just an occasional distant cry of the red kites.

"He's still there," said Maddie, the only one of us three who wasn't struggling to run and breathe at the same time.

"I know," I muttered. "Keep going."

"What if …?"

"He won't."

"I wish I knew what was going on."

"I will tell you," I gasped painfully. "Get to the field."

My pace was faltering but Maddie ran ahead and I didn't want her to reach the field first. Not from any stupid competitive reason – I just needed to be the one to face John Barleycorn.

We turned down the farm track. Sweat was running into my eyes and my throat hurt, bringing back horrible memories of school cross-country runs. The kites were in the air, but flying separately, making high circles and spirals over the centre of the field.

We had to slow down. The track was dry and rutted with long days of no rain. We paced along the field margin until we were roughly halfway down.

Evan had slowed down too. He was struggling even more than we were. I suppose I had something of an advantage in that I hadn't just been beaten heavily with a walking stick.

There was a parallel line of flattened crops running from where we were, out into the middle of the field. And it led straight to the now-standing figure of John Barleycorn.

The wooden handle of the sickle was warm in my sweaty hand. I lifted it up slightly.

"You two need to stay here," I said.

"I don't think so," Maddie said.

"Nope. Not gonna happen." Ceri folded her arms and did her very best "I am a mother and therefore I am in charge" facial expression, which to be fair was pretty effective. "We've come this far with you. Maddie needs to go with you because she has magic, and I need to come with her because I am not gonna stand here with that prick." She nodded at the wheezing Evan.

"Mom!"

"Well, it's true," she said.

"I've never heard you swear before!"

"That's because you don't listen," Ceri retorted automatically.

I rolled my eyes. "Come *on* then." Before I started down the tractor-path, I pointed the sickle at Evan. Actually it's not that easy to threaten someone with the point of a sickle because of its curved shape, but I did wiggle it menacingly at him. "You stay right there. Or you know what I'll do to you."

He didn't argue.

I set off along the flattened wheel-rut. Snatches of songs rose in my throat now I had got enough breathe back to countenance singing. I hummed and to my right hand side, Maddie hummed too. She didn't need to know the songs because the Fair Folk would sing them through her, and she would draw strength from that.

The oats danced their hairy heads to each side of us. Really this should have been a barley field, but I didn't think the scarecrow up ahead of us was going to be too bothered. I'd been trying to balance the unbalanced, trying to close the circle but as Gruffydd had said to me, it's not that simple. It never is. Yin and yang's a fine idea but we're never so evenly matched in reality.

I raised the sickle high in front of me as I approached and a curious feeling of respect washed through me. "Sir John!"

He raised his hand in acknowledgment but he remained on his feet. He would not kneel or bow for me to take my shot at him. He was a king, after all.

A sir, a king, a man, a symbol, and a sacrifice.

He was almost fully human-looking now. I stopped a few feet in front of him and felt very nervous. If he had still looked like a scarecrow, all clumsy stuffing and humorous face, this next act would have been far easier.

But now he was a tall, straight-standing man with his feet planted shoulder-width apart. His fabric face had filled out and taken on real features. There was the glint of an eye under his deep brows. He put his hands on his hips and waited.

"Oh god, oh no," I whispered. "I can't do this."

He grinned.

I wasn't strong enough. I wasn't brave enough. Dilys could beat hell out of a man with her stick but this – no, not this. I had to chop his legs off with my sickle and I nearly dropped it, my damp hand was shaking that much. He was too real.

"Bron?" Maddie said. "What do you need to do?"

"I need to kill him," I said, and the words broke in my mouth. I'd never said such a thing before. I'd never said such a thing in truth before.

"No, surely you can..."

"It has to be done. It's symbolic."

"Then do it symbolically," she said. "You know, tap his knee…"

I could tell that she was as bothered by his reality as I was. But then Ceri, on my other side, spoke. Her voice was harder. "Bron, you need to do this. You are your mother's daughter."

At first I thought that was a terrible thing to say. After all that I had learned about my mother, it wasn't something that I wanted to be reminded of. Then I realised what she meant.

My mother could help. Not that evil essence that lingered in the dead willow's heart, but her whole self – the good and bad, messed up, mixed up, real self that we all are.

"But she's too far away," I said. "I never did find her in the Otherworld. She's passed on, and she's gone."

"She's right here, you idiot," Ceri said.

So I called her. I didn't call loudly or over a great distance. I whispered it, calling within myself, for all that had made me into who I was now. I pleaded for her help, her courage and her strength.

Spirals, not circles; I was calling on my own self, of course, but more than that, rising, falling, an endless turning of the energy, an ouroboros of self-fulfilling and self-feeding power.

Things had to rebound, reverse and rebut. I tried to be good, and light, and warm and nice but these traits were of no use now. Except that by being bad I was going to be good. Oh, what did that even mean?

I gathered up my darkness and my pain and my sorrow and my anger and all of the negativity of my mother and my feelings around her and I strode forward, two long strides, and brought the sickle around from the right in a low arc and aimed not at his legs but at a point beyond his legs. I pushed right on through and the blade shimmered keenly through the straw like it was nothing, the yellow stalks and the fabric of his jeans offering no resistance at all, a magical act truly.

I hadn't realised my eyes had been closed until I opened them again.

There was nothing there but a pile of straw.

Twenty-two

"It's over," said Maddie.

I closed my eyes again.

"It's not over," Ceri said in a small voice now.

There was a hole deep within me and I looked into it. It was a bottomless well. You could fill it and fill it and it would always be empty. *I might as well lie down,* I thought. *I might as well sleep. I might as well sleep for ever, you know. The earth would be my bed, and I would welcome the dark embrace.*

I pitched forwards.

Ceri screamed, and Maddie grabbed me. She knelt in front of me and tried to prise my eyes open with her fingers. "Bron, Bron, wake up!"

"I need to sleep," I slurred. "For ever."

It was not a lack of magic or of power or of energy. Maybe it was an over-abundance of it, I don't know. I just longed for nothingness, emptiness, a lack of any demands upon me. Hadn't I earned that?

I heard Evan crying.

That stirred me. I forced my heavy eyelids up and saw him

behind Ceri. He had wrapped his arms around himself and he was sobbing. He looked, for all the world, like a little boy in desperate need of a hug.

Supported by Maddie, I got to my feet and approached him. I couldn't rest yet. The sickle lay on the ground but he still eyed me with anxiety. "It's okay," I said to him.

He was bawling now. He wasn't well, he wasn't well in the head; he was split open and he was hurting. I didn't think I could put him back together again, but I offered him my hand. "What's it all been about, Evan?"

"Her. You. Ruining everything."

"But Evan, you weren't even around when Ceri and my mam were living here in Llanfair."

"He was though. Mr Rigby."

Benedict Rigby. *Mister* Rigby? "Evan, you grew up here, right?"

"Yeah."

He was bow-shouldered, head-lowered, a picture of dejection. I didn't need to say anything more. I knew. I *knew*. Here was a little lost boy of a man who had found his role model and his whole purpose in Benedict Rigby so many years ago, and like a million other vulnerable people, he'd doted on someone who had given his life meaning.

Everything Evan did was for Benedict Rigby, a man I'd never met. A man who'd started this little magical group, for whatever reason – that hardly mattered. A man who'd written some esoteric texts and had inspired such devotion. He did it for him, and for the memory of him, the one thing that Evan could cling to.

Evan had always vowed to avenge him.

He'd got it all wrong. There was no point in trying to explain it to him. I imagined that John and even Owain had tried, but Evan needed clarity and I understood that need. Evan had a fixed idea.

And he still had it.

He lunged at Ceri.

She stepped back. Maddie flung up her hands and shouted, "Stop!" Some light silver bells tinkled in the air and he batted at invisible flies that buzzed around his head.

"It's not over," I said. "Evan, you're coming with us."

"Where?" everyone asked.

I was already making my unsteady way along the tractor-rut. "To the barrow, of course. To where this all started. He said it wasn't a circle but this is something that *does* need to close."

***

We walked. It was a strange alliance, an uneasy truce. The four of us walked slowly, and Maddie began to ask questions. "First of all," she said. "Who said it wasn't a circle? What isn't a circle? What does it mean?"

"Gruffydd," I said, and wondered if by saying his name I would conjure him to appear at the barrow. He'd know. He'd know what was going on. "I think he meant that things weren't so neat and tidy. I have been looking for a way to restore balance but I might have been looking for the wrong thing."

"Uh-huh. Okay, next up. Why did you chop the legs off the scarecrow?" she asked.

"Oh, that is even easier to answer." I began to sing this time, not hum. I sang to her of the three men that came out of the west, and the character of little Sir John who was cut down in his prime. She listened and she understood.

"It's the harvest," she said at last.

"It's always a harvesting," I said. "In the end."

I sang the song again, and then we all fell silent. I could hear amplified music coming from the town centre but we trudged on, following a well-trodden footpath to cut across a sheep field. We followed a ridge up and over which opened out to the wide flat bowl-like valley, and there in the centre was the barrow standing on the top of the hill in the middle.

This was the ridge on which I'd seen Gruffydd standing.

We left the path now, and went directly across the grass towards the hump of the barrow. The red kites had left us and there was nothing in the brilliant blue sky but the high white plumes left by the jets of holidaymakers or the fighters from the RAF base over on Anglesey. The air around us was heavy and even the few insects that were flying seemed languid and their buzzing was low on effort.

There were no other sounds now but our footsteps and our breathing. The merriment of the town was long behind us.

We felt very remote and cut-off, all of a sudden. I think that Ceri and Maddie discerned it too, as they drew closer to me.

Supporting me, or wanting comfort from me?

Either was fine.

We reached the barrow. I faced the blank yawning blackness of the opening between the grey stones.

"I am so totally not going in there, you know," Maddie said. "Not in a million years."

"I wouldn't ask you to. No one's going in. I've sealed it."

"What with?"

"Magic."

"Right, sure." Maddie put out her hand and extended her fingertips towards the entrance. She suddenly drew them back as if she'd been stung. "Oh yeah. I see. Nice work."

"Thanks. I'm also available for domestic security, securing one's car, and general incarceration duties."

"Useful. I'll take your number."

Our banter, short and stupid though it was, made my belly feel warm. Our relationship was back and it was a reassuring strength.

Ceri understood and I caught a glimpse of her smile.

Evan, however, did not get it at all. He'd never had such a connection with another person. He was frowning, and his face was twisted up in a pale mash of anxiety and anger and fear. He hovered close to us, and stared only at me.

I'd become an obsession for him. He was a man who needed obsessions. He needed a focus and now that focus was me, and bringing me "back" to his little group of magicians. Oh, and "getting even" with Ceri.

I turned away from him and approached the willow. It was a shocking sight of deadness in an otherwise green and fertile scene – even the stones of the barrow looked more alive than this thing. I put my hands on the too-cold bark and opened my awareness to what lingered, festering, deep inside.

"You came back to me!" the nasty voice cackled.

"There is no 'you' and I do not recognise you." I cloaked myself in a mental cape of grey and the absence of colour; I tried not to consider this a banishing ritual but I suppose that it was, and these were usually ill-advised. But it was necessary, whatever the cost.

I supposed that Ceri knew all about that.

But if I lost my power doing this …

No. I shut out the negative thoughts, and got on with my task.

I walked around the tree widdershins, then sunwise, winding and unwinding. I took off my shoes at the north quarter, and I ran my fingers through my hair at the south, a symbolic unbraiding, my hair being too short to actually be undone.

I cast off and cast out and rejected that essence and I began to hum, a flat note, tuneless, devoid of all meaning as I walked and turned and walked again. I spun a net then broke it apart. I made nothing but holes and gaps. I unmade it all.

Then I came to a halt and put my hands back on the tree again, and the energy that I had gathered discharged in a sudden loud crack and I jumped back with an involuntary cry.

The willow now was split wide open. Its two halves were twisted and fallen away from the centre.

It was empty.

The final remnants of the trapped essence of the bad decisions my mother made – they dissipated. There was not a trace of them remaining.

I liked to think that this meant she was finally fully free.

As was I. Or I would be, in time.

Evan fell to his knees and he was crying again. Ceri and Maddie turned to watch him. Ceri had horror on her face, but Maddie was a genuinely lovely person and she felt no awkwardness now in going to his side. She hunkered down next to him and put her hand on the back of his neck. She glanced up at me.

I came to stand in front of them.

She had questions on her face.

I crouched, too. I put my hand on Evan's shoulder. "Benedict Rigby showed you kindness and gave you a way to live your life, didn't he? He gave you a kind of framework, a path to follow, that made sense to you, made sense of the chaos."

"I am a chaos magician…"

"I don't think that you are," I said. "It's a fancy word but it's not who or what you are. I think you have a lot more learning to do. But you stopped learning when Rigby died. There is more to find out, you know. You go by what he told you but now he's not here, you have to keep on learning and … you have to make your own decisions. Especially now you don't have the Book of Dooms any longer."

I paused. "And, uh, sorry about that, by the way. It honestly was an accident. Anyway." I looked up at Ceri. "It's time we told everyone everything, isn't it?"

She nodded slowly. "I guess."

"Stop me if I get any of this wrong." I had one free hand

and I put it on Maddie's shoulder before I started. "Okay. So my mam was the older one, and auntie Ceri was the younger, and my mam left home before Ceri even got to school."

Ceri nodded.

"By the time that Ceri got to her late teens and felt a power rising in her, my mam was already involved with Benedict Rigby and his particular brand of magic."

Maddie narrowed her eyes. "But Bron…"

"And I won't say they were evil but they did some things I'd consider bad. And because of their influence and my own mother's weakness they tried to take Ceri's power."

"And my weakness," Ceri said. "I could not stand up to them properly."

"No, but you did," I said. "You sought help. The polecat was an animal guide and you knew enough to trust it. I wish Horatio had been around then. But instead you spoke with the other man at the church. And you ended up promising to destroy her."

Ceri bit her lip. Maddie shuddered.

"But you didn't. You didn't, see. You used every scrap of your untrained power and trapped all of my mam's magic in that willow tree. By doing that, you saved her."

"But she never forgave me," Ceri said.

"Is that why you left for America?" Maddie asked.

"Yeah, pretty much. It's been my home ever since. For far longer than I ever lived here."

Maddie looked at the bowed head of Evan. "And this guy?"

"He knew that someone had trapped my mam's magic and

he wanted revenge. It was written in their book. Some people always need someone else to blame for what's wrong in their life. For Evan, that was … Ceri. She was the target of all his anger."

"She still is," he hissed, finally raising his head. "I will get even."

"No, it's over."

That voice came from behind me. I saw shock on Evan's face. He stiffened under my hand. I recognised it was Gruffydd.

"You took your time," I said.

TWENTY-THREE

Evan tried to get to his feet but he was drained, both physically and emotionally. He staggered, and Gruffydd caught him, using one arm around his waist to hold him up. Evan half-heartedly fought against him, but the blacksmith was a stubborn and solid wall.

"What are you going to do with him?" Maddie asked.

"I'm going to help him," Gruffydd said. "I'll take him back to the forge and put the kettle on."

I winced. "You don't clean your mugs. How will dysentery help him?"

He didn't rise to my weak joke.

Maddie said, "Why would you help him? You're not … one of them, are you?"

"Of course not. I am not one of anyone. But then, of course, why would I *not* help him?"

"Because he …"

"Made some terrible decisions, just like everyone else does. Anyway, he looked after the barrow for me, more than anyone else. And that counts for something, you know. I am not so black and white, and nor are you, or any of you here. Stop forcing it all into boxes. I told you before."

Gruffydd began to walk away, half-carrying the limp form of Evan. I was pleased, actually, that Evan was in safe hands. He was a pathetic figure.

"What about the barrow now?" Ceri asked.

He raised up his free hand, but carried on walking.

"What does that mean?" Ceri demanded.

"I think it just means he's got it under control," I said.

"Right."

He didn't stop walking but he did call back over his shoulder, "Oh and by the way, Dilys's scarecrow has won some sort of prize. You ought to go and congratulate her."

"And apologise to the judges," I replied.

"Wow, do you think she used magic? Maybe she charmed them or something," Maddie said.

"The last we saw of her, she was heading into the café to drink all of Alston's hidden alcohol."

Maddie's eyes widened in genuine alarm. "What are we doing here? We had better get back."

Ceri and Maddie linked arms, and began to walk away. I lingered, and looked at the barrow and the willow.

I felt sad, but lightened too.

I wanted everything to be back to normal, but everything had changed, and I felt older. I suppose that I felt more like a grown-up, in some ways. Not all, though. I don't believe that ever really happens, like Dilys had pointed out to me.

I followed along behind Ceri and Maddie, an unshakeable mother-daughter unit, and I was glad for them.

TWENTY-FOUR

The market place was a festive place, full of laughing crowds, photographers, families, scarecrows, musicians and food smells. We pushed our way through and reached Caffi Cwtch. It was busy but there was no sign of Dilys nor her confederates Jemima and Billy.

"Oh god, no," I said, as a horrible suspicion dawned on me. "Maybe they've gone on a pub crawl."

"It's the middle of the afternoon," Maddie pointed out, then she stopped and thought about it. "Yeah, but Dilys though. So, maybe. We should alert Adam."

Alston saw us dithering by the door. He shouted over the heads of the customers waiting at the till, to their surprise and annoyance. "Are you after that mad aunt of yours? I had to ask her to leave. I can't have that kind of talk here. She'd clot the cream, she would, that one, with that mouth on her."

"I am so sorry."

"And she owes me eight pound seventy and a bowl of sugar lumps. Munched her way right through the lot, she did. Surprised she's got any teeth."

"She hasn't. Okay, I'll come by and settle up when I've got some cash," I assured him. "Where did she go?"

"Home, I hope. I don't know. I don't care. She needs to learn that napkins are not suitable for origami, and *that* sort of origami is not suitable in a family-friendly establishment."

Outside we were greeted by Harkin, who was being petted by a small girl who had accidentally got her sticky half-sucked lollipop stuck in his fur. I prised it out and was about to tell her to rinse it off but she shoved it straight into her mouth and toddled off to her waiting mother.

Harkin wove around my legs, happily purring. There was an air of settled contentment about the cat, and he was pulling me home.

"I think we'll find Dilys back at the house," I said. "Harkin is feeling all domestic and nesty, if you see what I mean."

It would have been nice, perhaps, to soak up the carnival atmosphere a little more, but we were all tired. I was also hungry and I guessed that the others would be, too.

Sure enough, when we walked through the back door and utility room, we found Great Aunt Dilys waiting for us in the kitchen. She was sitting at the table, and she had a small arrangement of corn dollies in front of her. These were not doll-shaped corn dollies. They were the traditional type, twisted loops with a fan of straw below them, tightly plaited and particularly hard-wearing.

"Is everything settled now?" she asked.

I met Ceri's eyes. There was one thing yet to be said. But I nodded. "Yeah."

"Go on."

"You can surely guess it all."

"Humour me. So who was behind it all?"

"Evan. Only Evan," I said.

"But the others knew and didn't stop him."

"That's true."

"Is he still a danger?"

"No."

"Are you sure?"

I smiled. "Gruffydd has him. I suspect that he is going to be thoroughly re-educated."

Maddie said, "You mean, Evan has a new Benedict Rigby."

"I hadn't thought of that." I sat down heavily on a wooden chair and Harkin jumped up into my lap. My fingers caught in the sticky patch of his fur. He began to groom. "But yes, I think so. Evan needs direction."

"From him?"

"Well, who else? Not me, that's for sure."

We all digested that possibility, and everyone agreed in a rush that yes, I would indeed be the worst person in the world to try and inspire a weak and vulnerable man who needed certainty in his life.

Dilys broke the meditation. She picked up one of the corn dollies and handed it to Maddie. I was given one, and then Ceri.

"Keep these with you," Dilys told us. "Keep these with you all year. It's important."

"Why?" I couldn't detect any magic around them.

"To remind you of what you've learned," Dilys pronounced.

"I've learned a bit about red kites," I retorted factitiously.

"Thank you, Dilys," Maddie said politely, and stuck her tongue out at me.

Ceri looked at the corn dolly. "There are rules about what you can and can't take into a foreign country," she said. "You know, about plants and things, that might upset the ecosystem. Do you think this will be okay to go through customs?"

I looked at Maddie in trepidation.

Maddie blinked. "Mom?"

"Maddie, I need to go. This has been a great trip and all, but this isn't my home any more. I miss your dad, and he's probably running out of socks."

"Mom, he does more laundry than you do."

"Only because I tell him to."

"You've only been here five days."

"I know. And look, I've brought you into danger. I don't regret coming. These things that happened, they should have been put to rest a long time ago. But my part in it all is over now. I am – well, I was – the Unbalancer and I've done my bit. I've got to leave."

"When?"

"My flight is booked for tomorrow."

"Your flight?" Maddie said. "Not … our flight?"

"You don't want to come back to the US," Ceri said.

Maddie blinked. "No, you're right, I don't. Not yet, at any rate."

At that point I realised I'd been holding my breath. I let it out in a silent whoosh.

Maddie continued. "I've got things to do here, right?"

I grinned. "Yeah, well, Sian can't do without you. You're halfway through that course on the Welsh language – can you even say hello yet, properly? And Harkin would miss you terribly."

"Yeah, yeah, all that," she answered with a laugh. "But more importantly, you know, someone needs to sort out your pigheaded stupid relationship out."

"Excuse me?"

"You heard. Honestly. I want to blame you and I really kinda do but if I don't step in, Adam will spend the rest of his life sulking in his house and working himself to death, and you will … well, you'll just be you, but even grumpier."

Dilys shook a corn dolly at me. "And nobody wants that, do they?"

No. I guess they didn't.

Maddie enfolded me in a tight hug and I held her for longer than I needed to. Just in case she squirmed away and jumped on that plane after all.

***

It was an emotional farewell to Ceri. I suddenly wanted to beg her to stay, just a little longer, and tell me all about my mother.

But that would have caused us both pain in the long run.

I stood off to one side as Maddie and Ceri spent their last moments together at the airport. Then Ceri disappeared through the gates, and Maddie remained on her own for five minutes, as crowds flowed around her and announcements came over the tannoy in a multiplicity of languages.

She wasn't crying when she came back to me, though she had been. "Am I making the right decision?" she asked.

"Yes, if you are about to say we should go get a drink before we hop on the bus to get home."

"No. I mean, staying."

"Of course you are. You've got things to finish."

"I'm scared of ending up like my mom."

"You're like a more sensible version of her, so there's no danger of that."

She smiled. "I know. No, I mean, she's kinda rootless now. She's not American and she's not Welsh. She's been too long there to come back here but…"

"Isn't America some glorious melting pot of immigration and identity?" I said.

She narrowed her eyes at me. "Yes, it's a constant joyous dancing musical of tolerance and acceptance," she said.

"Ouch, you are not usually sarcastic."

"And that's the thing," Maddie went on. "I'm getting more British. I said 'mate' to someone the other day in the shop. What if I stay here too long and can't go home?"

"I don't think your visa will let you," I said.

She sighed.

"I'm sorry," I went on. "I don't know. I don't think there's a definite timeline and one day you'll wake up and a switch has gone off and boom! You can't be Californian any longer. It doesn't work like that and I honestly don't think you need to worry. Unless…"

"Unless what?" We began walking through the concourse and out to the shuttle bus terminal that would take us onwards to another bus, and another, a long journey over the border back to Wales.

"Well," I said. "There's Owain."

"Oh my gosh no!

"Steady on now. He's sweet. He's a poet. He's not really one of them. And he likes you."

"No," she said, more seriously. "Not after everything. What about you and Adam?"

"I know, I know, I'm on it." Something jogged my memory. An unpleasant little comment that Evan had made. "Maddie, do you think that John had … has … a thing for me."

"The red kite man? Wow. Um, no, Bron. That would be ridiculous."

"Why so? Am I not likeable?"

"Shut up," she said. "You two are too similar."

I didn't reply to that. I was taken aback. I didn't want to probe that any further.

I looked up at the message board over the bus shelters. They flickered and I screened myself. "We've got thirty minutes yet."

"Quick drink, then?"

I grinned. "More British by the day, you. Yes, come on."

The End

Thank you for reading! This is the fifth book in the series (although you can read them in any order really). The others are:

What The Cat Dragged In
Playing Cat And Mouse
All Cats Are Grey in The Dark
Raining Cats And Dogs

I have a weekly newsletter if you are interested in folklore, herbal chit chat and so on. But I'm not joking – it's every Friday – so if you're suffering under a slew of mailing lists, do think carefully about signing up. If you definitely want to be pestered by me, just type this into your browser.

http://www.subscribepage.com/n8z7a5

I am on Facebook here and usually around for a chat. https://www.facebook.com/MollyMilliganAuthor/

If you could leave a review, I'd be very grateful.